THE PAPER MAN

A DEBUT NOVEL BY

DAVID JAMES ROBERTS

BLUE FORGE PRESS
Port Orchard ✹ Washington

Blue Forge Press is the print division of the volunteer-run, federal 501(c)3 nonprofit, Blue Legacy (EIN 83-4307421), founded in 1989 and dedicated to supporting artisans marginalized due to race, age, disability, economics or other factors. We strive to empower storytellers from all walks of life with our four divisions: Blue Forge Press, Blue Forge Films, Blue Forge Gaming, and Blue Forge Sound. Find out more at www.BlueForgeGroup.org

Blue Forge Press
7419 Ebbert Drive Southeast
Port Orchard, Washington 98367
blueforgepress@gmail.com
360-550-2071 ph.txt

Blue Forge Press
7419 Ebbert Drive Southeast
Port Orchard, Washington 98367
blueforgepress@gmail.com
360-550-2071 ph.txt

For Kristina, you are my smile, my heart, my life. You make all my dreams come true. I love you forever.

For Gabriella, you are my superhero!

For my mom, thank you for your love, support and guidance through this project. I could not have done it without you.

ACKNOWLEDGEMENTS

I wish to thank the many people who've inspired me and helped me on the amazing journey of completing this book. They include, but are not limited to; William Alspaugh, Dana Barney, Larry Lucken, the good people at The Tacoma Public Library, and the countless people who've inspired me throughout my life.

THE PAPER MAN

A DEBUT NOVEL BY

DAVID JAMES ROBERTS

PREFACE

In March of 1938, the world lost a nation.

Austria and Germany unified as one nation in an event known as the Anschluss. It was not a seamless moment in history.

Austria, the nation of Hitler's birth, was experiencing a period of governmental turmoil. The nation's Chancellor, Kurt Alois Josef Johan Schuschnigg, was weak and corrupt. The nation was poor and still reeling from the end of World War I, a war it lost along with Germany. Throughout the decades after the war, Austria saw a number of violent conflicts between different political groups, including anarchists, religious fundamentalists, communists, socialists, and fascists. Schuschnigg struggled not only to hold his nation together, but he also struggled to hold onto his power.

Austria's neighbor to the north was already stirring the winds of war and expanding its borders. Adolf Hitler, the Nazi dictator was threatening to invade Austria unless a Nazi-sympathetic government was installed. Schuschnigg scoffed at Hitler's taunts and turned to his friend and ally, Benito Mussolini, the fascist dictator of Italy.

Il Duce threatened to go to war with Germany if Hitler followed through with his threat to invade. Instead, the Fuhrer staged a massive propaganda campaign inside Austria to bring as many people to his side as possible. He then called for a vote, a referendum of sorts, asking the Austrian people a simple question, do you or do you not support Hitler and the Nazi party.

Despite clear evidence of ballot-box stuffing and voter intimidation, the final tally showed that the Austrians overwhelmingly supported the Nazis, with ninety percent voting yes. Seeing the final "official" tally, Mussolini dropped his objections and Hitler used the results as an excuse to unify the two nations.

Only two nations voiced opposition to the Anschluss, Mexico and The U.S.S.R.

Many Austrians, mostly the rich, tried to emigrate in fear for their lives and safety. Those who were not able to join opposition groups or kept their opposition to themselves.

Schuschnigg was forced to resign from the chancellorship. In his farewell speech, he issued a dire plea to his fellow Austrians:

"I take leave of the Austrian people with a German word of farewell, uttered from the depth of my heart, God protect Austria."

Hitler deputized one of his disciples, Adolf Eichmann to deal with the Austrian Jews. At the time of the Anschluss, Austria had a Jewish population of approximately 190,000. It was up to Eichmann to expel, deport, or make life so miserable for the Jews that they would regret not having left long before the takeover of their nation.

To commemorate the Anschluss "victory," Hitler called for a celebratory soccer match to be played between the German National Team and the Austrian National Team. It was to be the last time the Austrian National Team would ever play together as Austrians. In all future international soccer competitions, the best players from Austria would play alongside the Germans as Germany.

Soccer was one of the most popular sports in Austria in the 1920s and 1930s and the Austrian National Team was one of the best in the world. That team's best player and the captain was a man named Matthias Sindelar. Between April 1931 and December 1932, he led the National Team on an unprecedented fifteen game unbeaten streak. The streak earned the team the monicker, "Das Wunderteam." Even though Sindelar never led the team to win a World Cup (a tournament run by soccer's international governing body, the Federation International de Football Association, or FIFA), his impact on the game was unsurpassed for its time. He helped pave the way for more of the game's legends. Legends like Brazil's Pele, Germany's Franz Beckenbauer, and Argentina's Diego Maradona.

Sindelar was a star on and off the soccer pitch. Because of unrivaled athletic genius, the press nicknamed him The Mozart of Football and Der Papierene, or The Paper Man.

PART I

"The excitement unleashed whenever the white bullet makes the net ripple might appear mysterious or crazy, but remember the miracle doesn't happen very often. The goal, even if it be a little one, is always a gooooooal in the throat of the commentators, a 'do' sung from the chest that would leave Caruso forever mute, and the crowd goes nuts and the stadium forgets that it's made of concrete and breaks free of the earth and flies through the air."

—Eduardo Galeano, *Soccer in Sun and Shadow*

A mouse huddled itself by the steps of the Ring Cafe. It nibbled on the still-warm crumbs of cakes and pastries the customers had dropped. As it reached out with its little hands for whatever it could eat in these last days of winter, it was oblivious to the horrors in the rest of the world around it.

The branches of the trees had not yet budded leaves. People walking along the boulevards could still see their breath float away in the air. Some people welcomed the coming of spring, others saw the winter as lasting an eternity. The period between winter and spring was a season distinct in itself. It was a season of contradiction. It was a season of fear. It was a season of hope. It was a season of dread. It was a season of weakness. It was a season of strength.

The city of Vienna would never be the same again after this season ended and the next began. The customers of the Ring Cafe, as well as the rest of the Viennese, would be divided over how they saw this change. The city of art and science was the treasured pearl of Central Europe. But now, the Austrian capital was under the dominion of Adolf Hitler's Germany. The image of the German dictator was seemingly everywhere. Flying on banners across the great opera houses and classical architecture of the city. Hanging above the mantelpieces and credenzas of the restaurants and cafes. On lampposts and storefronts, people showed support for the Anschluss by hanging signs and posters of his portrait, letting everyone know that he was coming. Under his mustached face, the German word for yes, "Ja!" Even though those who supported the Anschluss were born Austrians, they now saw themselves as Germans and wanted Hitler to be their leader. Those who opposed the Anschluss were silenced, one way or another. Those who did not want to be beaten up or worse simply kept their thoughts to themselves.

As the mouse supped on his crumbs, a group of young men dressed in brown clothes with white leggings, a symbol of Nazi solidarity amongst the Austrian youth, stood near a flagpole in front of the Ring. One of them lowered the Austrian flag while the others smoked cigarettes. One was holding a bright red flag. Once the Austrian flag was completely lowered and unhinged from the pole's line, he handed the red flag, the swastika-emblazoned Nazi flag, to his friend for it to be raised instead over the Austrian capital.

The maitre d' of the Ring stepped out of the cafe

with a broom. He was about to shoo away the mouse with it when he looked up and saw the boys. He gently shook his head and began to sweep the critter away from the cafe. The mouse, now frightened for his life, ran for safety. His meal was over.

Taking a deep breath, the maitre d' looked up and a smile came over his clean-shaven face. A tall, handsome man walked towards him. His blonde hair, mostly covered by a Fedora, was cut neatly. his overcoat was freshly cleaned and pressed. His gait was long and confident. The maitre d' recognized him instantly.

"Der Paperiene!" he shouted excitedly. "You look American!"

With a tip of his hat, he smiled at the maitre d'. He was Matthias Sindelar. He was more than just a celebrity. He was a superstar. To his fans, he was a footballing god. He was the stand-out player for the Austrian National Team and the Vienna-based football club Austrian Wien. He played the game gracefully and made the game look easy.

The press nicknamed him Der Paperiene, or the Man of Paper, because of his thin build and gentle face. When he played, some described him as having the elegance of a piece of paper floating on the wind. Another nickname he earned was the Mozart of Football because of his innate genius for the game. He could score with ease.

With merely his toe, he could make the ball do more than other players could using their entire foot. The way he dismantled a defense was the same way a matador humbled a bull. With grace, finesse, and ruthlessness.

"The Americans might be able to tailor a fine suit," as he touched the lapel of his imported Brooks Brothers jacket, "but I doubt they can bake Sachertorte properly," he responded as he strutted past.

"I'll make sure to save a slice just for you, Sindi!"

"I'll be by later this afternoon!" he said with a smile.

His smile faded quickly though. He saw the young Nazi sympathizers. They had already raised their flag, now they were circled around a young teenage girl. They had her cornered in front of an alleyway.

Matthias' heart raced and ached for her. Her eyes were fixed on the ground as she tried to shield herself any way she could from their unwanted advances. The boys ran their fingers through her hair and down her cheek. Every time she raised her arms for protection, they pulled her arm down.

Matthias rushed over to the girl.

"Abigail!" he said loudly. The boys stopped and looked at him. "Are these boys bothering you?"

The girl froze in confusion but quickly she realized that he was trying to help her. She gave a gentle nod.

"Move along old man, this doesn't concern you!" one of the boys shouted.

"This is my niece and her mother is probably worried sick about her," Matthias said. He reached out for her, took her arm in his hand, and pulled her away from the boys. "You run home and tell my sister I'll be by later."

The girl started to walk away with great haste. One of the boys squinted his eyes at Matthias.

"Aren't you..." he began to ask.

"No, I get that all the time. Now get out of here before I tell your parents."

The boys started to walk away. One of them turned around, rose his arm in the air in the Nazi salute, and shouted, "Austria is kaput!"

Matthias looked at them and shook his head in disappointment.

Matthias longed to retire. He was on the wrong side of 30 by five years. His glory days were mostly behind him. He wanted to retire peacefully. The life of a celebrity was starting to wear on him mentally. He told himself that he wanted to be able to enjoy a visit to a cafe or a restaurant without being recognized. Yet, almost ironically, in his heart of hearts, he still loved being recognized and receiving the adulation.

But peacefulness eluded him. His enemy was no longer directly in front of him on the soccer pitch. He was fighting something deeper than another player wearing a different colored uniform. Now the fight was against a mentality, a belief, a way of life.

Ever since Hitler began his proverbial saber-rattling to unify Germany and Austria, it was as if a strange mist had descended upon everyone. Hatred was everywhere. Suspicion lurked around every corner. And fear was so prevalent, it felt inescapable.

For Matthias, Vienna was home. When walking through the streets, he never tired of the sight of the architecture honoring the heroes of old. Windows housed inside arches, with artful flourishes as if they were directly inspired by one of Mozart's symphonies, graced the ancient boulevards lining the city. Even though he saw these inspiring sights throughout most of his adult life, he never tired of them. The design of the city filled him with comfort which truly made him feel like he was where he was supposed to be.

As a professional soccer player, he traveled throughout greater Europe and visited many of the continent's greatest cities. Paris, London, Rome, Munich, Edinburgh, Prague, and many others. But whenever he returned to Vienna from his travels, he felt centered.

Yet, even in this dark hour, now that banners with

swastika flags flew everywhere and posters with Hitler's face were plastered on any bare wall, Vienna still made him feel at home.

On the streets of Vienna and throughout Austria, people walked around as if nothing was the matter. Matthias sometimes wondered to himself if people were merely pretending that the actions of the government in Berlin were of no matter to them. People still stopped to say hello to an old friend, as long as that friend was not a Jew.

One of the most popular cafes, and a favorite of Matthias, was the Ring. It was designed to be a comfortable place for Vienna's bourgeoisie to mingle, gossip, and relax. The dining room was large enough to accommodate approximately one hundred people. Over their Viennese coffees, espressos, cappuccinos, and fancy pastries they discussed the issues of the day. Crystal glass chandeliers hung from the high vaulted ceiling illuminating the booths and the banquettes row upon row. The windows looked out on the city street. To some, it was merely a fancy coffee house. To others, it was a hub, a cross-section, of art and politics.

Matthias was scheduled to meet the national team manager, Heinrich Retschury, there for a coffee. Retschury had taken over managerial duties for the team following the death of long time skipper Hugo Meisl. The new coach dearly wanted his star forward to play in the upcoming "celebratory" Anschluss Match.

The coach was already there waiting when Sindelar arrived. As soon as the player walked through the door, he removed his Fedora. He handed his hat and scarf to the maitre-d' and removed his coat. A few people in the cafe began to applaud as they recognized the icon.

He waved and gave a modest smile to his adoring fans as he spotted his coach. Retschury stood, greeting his player with a warm smile making the whiskers of his thin mustache spread and bristle. The two shook hands as Matthias pulled his chair out to sit. As the coach got comfortable again, he rubbed the tip of his forefinger and thumb over his mustache, putting the hairs back in place.

A waiter approached.

"Macchiato," Matthias said anticipating the question. "Doppio."

The waiter turned to Heinrich who shook his head softly.

"I'm fine," he said. "Thank you."

The waiter walked towards the kitchen. Heinrich picked up the crystallized sugar and stirred it into his espresso which he had been sipping since before Matthias arrived.

"I know you know why I asked you to meet me here," the coach said to his player.

Matthias crossed his legs, sat back, and crossed his arms over his chest.

"You want to convince me to play," he said with a half-grin on his face.

Both men were aware that Hitler had ordered the game between Germany and Austria. It would be the last time the Austrians would play as Team Austria. After the match ended, Hitler wanted the best Austrian players to play alongside the Germans as one team going forward. It was clear that the game was to be nothing more than propaganda.

"Why do you want me to play?"

"It will be your testimonial."

Matthias breathed deeply when he heard those words. A final match. Win, lose or draw, Matthias could say goodbye to his fans wearing the crest of his nation over his heart, not the crest of his nation's conquerors. Heinrich knew that by appealing to a player's ego he might well convince him to put on his cleats one last time. Once a player retires, they don't just miss hearing the roar of the crowd cheer for them after scoring a goal. They go into a state of mourning over it as if they had lost a loved one, knowing that this aspect of their life, a life that they had become identified with, was now officially over.

The waiter returned with Matthias's coffee. He also placed a slice of Sachertorte in front of the sports hero.

"Compliments of the house, Herr Sindelar," he said with a smile.

Matthias thanked the waiter as he picked up the coffee cup.

"The Reich wants to use this match to celebrate this," Heinrich said as he searched for the right words. He scrunched his face before saying, "Anschluss."

"What is there to celebrate? A few weeks ago we were Austrians, now we're Germans. Maybe next week we'll be Australians." He forced himself to hold back the mix of emotions he was feeling about the current state of national affairs. The resentment, the anger, the frustration, fear, and dejection were all brewing and simmering deep inside of him.

"Think of your fans, Sindi."

"Earlier today, I was taking my morning walk," he said slowly. "There was a group of young men, obviously eager to join the Hitlerjugend. They had this girl surrounded. She couldn't have been a day over fifteen. You could tell she was Jewish because of her clothes. The poor thing was frightened out of her mind about what they would do to her. And from the look on her face, she knew there was nothing that she could do about it because they would get away with it, too. Thankfully, I was there to help her before they could do anything." Matthias looked Heinrich directly in the eye. "This game is going to celebrate those scoundrels."

"Matthias," Heinrich searched for his next words carefully. "We're not like them. You and I, we're not like them."

The athlete pushed his coffee aside.

"I'm not a politician. I'm a footballer. I play football."

Heinrich smiled softly.

"Sports is politics," he said. "You are more popular than the mayor of Vienna. Our game, your teammates, the fans, me, we are all pawns in the games politicians play."

"Tell me the truth, Herr Trainer. Why do you want me to play? Seriously."

Heinrich sat back. His face softened.

"You are right, Matthias. The game is nothing more than political propaganda. Yes, it's being called a friendly, but we all know the truth. You can't even call it a sportsmanlike competition. The Nazis are even insisting that the game end in a draw."

Matthias's head tilted. He was shocked. His face showed that he was having trouble comprehending what the coach had just said.

"The result of the match is predetermined?" Matthias asked. "Who else knows this?"

"My assistant coaches, the coaching staff of Germany, and you. We're under orders to make sure the result is a tie."

"Why are we even," Matthias paused. "Why did we agree to play?"

"You ask that as if we even had a choice in the matter."

Matthias covered his gaping mouth with one hand. His stomach knotted with disgust at the thought of playing in a predetermined match.

"This isn't what football is about."

"I know."

"So, why ask me to play? If you want me there, I could put the ball in the back of the net regardless of what you order us to do from the touchline."

Heinrich leaned over the table. He wanted to make sure that Matthias heard him.

"I want you and our team to have its testimonial. I want every one of your teammates to go out with your heads held high. You have always been at the centerpiece of this team. You are Austrian football, Matthias! You lifted many trophies with Austria. Being out there would not just be for moral support. Your teammates and your fans would be able to applaud you and our nation's crest properly."

Matthias breathed deeply. His skipper's words were beginning to change his mind but he wasn't yet convinced.

"Are you going to tell the rest of the team? Surely, they can win without me there. They have in the past."

"I know. But, Sindi, your star burns brightest."

Matthias stared at the coach intently. His mind was full of conflicting thoughts about whether or not he should agree to play.

"What would you do if I score? What would you do if I score the winning goal in the final seconds of the game?"

"I'm not worried about the consequences," the coach said with a smirk and a twinkle in his eye. "The ball sometimes has a way to find its way into the net."

"It sounds like you want me to ignore their desire for this match to end in a tie."

"Matthias, I merely want you to play. I'm not the only one who wants to see you out there one more time."

The coach's face spoke the words that he genuinely wanted to say. He couldn't say what was in his heart because that would be too risky. The Nazis seemed to have spies everywhere and who knows what their hidden ears could hear.

He wanted to say to Matthias, "I want you to play because I know you'll score. I'll do everything I can to make it seem that you don't score. I'll play you out of position, I'll make you the goalkeeper, but, damn it, Matthias, you will still find a way to put the ball in the back of the net. I want you to play because Hitler will be at the game. I want to see his face when we beat him with all of the best players in the world. You are the best player ever. You have to be there."

But he didn't say those words. The look on his face did the talking for him.

The player read the words emblazoned on his coach's face. Matthias sat back in his chair. He looked around the dining room of the Ring. For a brief moment, he imagined seeing every seat in the Praterstadion filled, hearing the roar of the crowd cheering his name. He remembered the feeling he had whenever he heard their chants and songs. On that pitch, he was immortal. He was Apollo. He was Hercules. He was unstoppable.

He wanted to feel that way one more time.

The Praterstadion is not just a soccer stadium. It is a house of worship. It is where men become heroes or heroes become gods. It is the house where Matthias Sindelar, playing for both Austria Wien and the National Team, transformed himself from just another player into a god amongst men. When his boots touched the grass, and he put the ball through the goalmouth, the crowd roared his name into the heavens, directly into God's ears.

"Paparein! Paparein!"

"We love you, Sindi!"

His fans said he had brains in his legs. They described his playing ability as that of a ballerina. He was born in the Czech region of the Austria-Hungary Empire in the village of Kozlov. He was not born into a wealthy family. His father was a blacksmith who moved his family to Vienna when he was two years old hoping to find more work.

Young Matthias learned football playing in the streets of Vienna. He was fifteen when he became a professional. He was signed to Hertha Vienna. In 1924, he was sold to its cross-town rival, Austria Wien.

Sindelar's celebrity was not only due to his natural abilities with the ball. Blue-collar fans were drawn to him because of his working-class background. They saw themselves in him and looked up to him. They saw a boy from a small village who worked hard to harness his talent and turn it into a lucrative career. The upper classes, in turn, adopted him as one of their own. They did not shun him as "new money," instead, they saw a man who was a model of Austrian pride.

Matthias did not play sides when it came to issues dealing with class and social status. He had become wealthy, but never forgot where he had come from. He learned this lesson the hard way once.

As his celebrity began to rise, when he was in his early 20s, he started spending his riches on imported cigars, fancy cars, and fancier women. On the pitch, he also tended to be a showboat as he took matters into his own hands and routinely ignored the coach's directions. After a few too many warnings from the Austrian National Team's head coach, Hugo Meisl, Matthias was cut from the National Team's roster. Meisl hoped the decision would teach him a lesson in humility. Sindelar would not be invited back until he changed his ways.

"You're a goal scorer," Coach Meisl told Matthias when he gave him the news. "You know where you're supposed to put the ball and that means you're supposed to have an ego. But having an ego does not mean you're supposed to be egotistical. There is a bench full of players who want your spot. If you want to waste your God-given talent by doing what you're doing, by being egotistical, you can. But you won't be doing it on my team."

As he entered the world effectively exiled from international football, he took in the words of Meisl and he remembered the lesson his father taught him when he was a young boy. They were walking through the neighborhood of Leopoldstadt, a predominately Jewish area in Vienna. Young Matthias stared at the men with their long beards and curly payot hanging from their sideburns.

"Poppa, why are they dressed so strangely?"

"This is part of their culture."

"I think it's weird."

"Son, always remember this. Just because someone is different from you doesn't mean they are less than you or inferior. No matter who they are or where they come from. That man can change his hairstyle or change his shoes, but you and he drink the same water and breath the same air. Remember, we're all the same. We just show it differently."

"Why can't we all be the same?"

"That's not how God made us. He made us all different in different ways, the same in other ways. Do you know what one of those ways is, my son?"

"What's that?"

"We show kindness to others because it is the right thing to do."

Matthias thought about what his father told him and what his coach told him. He understood now that just because he was born with this ability, it didn't mean that he was owed anything. He was a better athlete but not a better person. He still had to prove himself on and off the field. He had to cultivate humility and earn people's gratitude and appreciation.

It took several years, but soon he earned his way back to the national team. It also helped that the Viennese sports press started bullying Coach Meisl to reinstate the young star. He stopped living like a carefree bachelor. With the national team, he competed in the 1934 World Cup which was held in Italy. While there, he met Camilla, an aspiring model who not only caught his eye, she also caught his heart.

The Austrian National Team was in Verona. On a day off, he and some teammates stopped in a random cafe. The Austrians sat down at a table next to which just happened to be another table where a group of young women was sitting. After exchanging glances with one another, Matthias leaned over and started a conversation with Camilla.

"I'm Matthias, I'm from Vienna," he said in broken Italian with a heavy accent.

"My name is Camilla," she replied. "I always wanted to see Vienna."

"I play football, but one day I'll probably open a cafe of my own." She smiled and chuckled at his joke. She found him charming and cute.

He was instantly in love and she was smitten. When he was not in Italy, he wrote to her. He paid her way to visit him in Austria and he made sure to meet her at the train station with a bouquet of flowers. In the offseason, he took her to a cabin in the Swiss Alps.

He knew he wanted to marry her, but she made it

clear that she was not quite ready to share him with football. So, he agreed that they would marry when he formally retired from the game. She moved to Vienna to be with him and waited for him to hang up the cleats and make a new life away from the world of sport.

The Praterstadion was where he played many games with the National Team. It was the home stadium for Austria Wien. On this chilly March afternoon, the cathedral of football was draped in the rays of the setting sun. Shadows cast by the pillars stretched over the cobblestone street. The door to the equipment office creaked open. Carrying a leather satchel, Dr. Michl Schwarz stepped through the doorway. He had served as president for Wien since 1910, and bringing Sindelar to the club was one of his proudest achievements.

As Michl left Wien's offices, he looked behind him, over his shoulder. The team's secretary, Egon Ulbrich, stood in front of the door to his office, two Nazi officials stood behind him. He was trying to hold back his tears. The last thing he wanted to do was let the Nazis know he was weak.

Michl walked out of the stadium and as he closed the heavy wooden door behind him, a wave of nostalgia swept over him. As he gazed at the Wien team crest, the club's initials inside a purple circle, the letter "A" being the largest and in the middle, he thought about the days when the only worry he had was whether or not Sindi would be healthy enough to play on game day. But those days were now long gone. He was upset that what was happening was something that he saw coming.

He left the letter he had just received that morning on his desk. As Egon handed him the letter, his hand shook with fear and sorrow. His voice cracked and he struggled to say the words he was ordered to say.

"Herr Doctor," he said. His throat was filled with the urge to cry. "I'm so sorry to have to say this. But I'm afraid your time here at Wien is ended."

With the seal of the party, an eagle atop a swastika, in the letterhead, it said that he had twelve hours to vacate the club. He was one of many Jewish soccer officials across Austria who received letters just like this one. He did not put up a fight as he read it. He listened stoically to the explanation from the officials. Germany now ruled Austria. All Jewish influence in all sporting activities was illegal. All sporting organizations, both professional and amateur, had to purge from its ranks all Jews. Players, administrators, secretaries, everyone. No one was exempt. Michl would not be compensated for his significant financial investments. His decades of devoted service and talent and hard work would be vacated and essentially ignored. He simply had to collect all his personal belongings, sign overall ownership of the club to someone chosen by the party and leave.

"Thank you, Egon," Michl responded, placing his hand on his shoulder. "I understand. Please know, this is not your fault. I am not angry with you."

As he ran his fingertips over the metal bolts on the door, he found the handle and gently guided it closed. He slowly put the key into the hole, knowing he would never close up the office again, and felt it latch. The sound of the lock taking struck his heart like a nail. He pursed his lips as he swallowed his fury to stop himself from crying. It was a hard fact for him to accept. Michl took a deep breath and forced himself to put one foot in front of the other and walk away from the stadium that he helped to build.

As he walked away from the life he knew, he heard a familiar voice calling for him.

"Herr Doctor!"

Michl turned around and saw Matthias coming towards him.

"Sindi! So nice to see you."

Michl quickly composed himself as Matthias approached. They shook hands and smiled at each other.

"Where are you heading to?" Matthias asked.

"Home. I thought you were meeting with Herr Retschury."

"He and I just spoke. I'm glad that I caught you. I was hoping to get your opinion on this matter."

Michl nodded his head and smiled. He was not happy, but he did not want to burden his friend. Nonetheless, it was impossible to hide his thoughts.

"Is something the matter?" Matthias asked.

"Wien and I have parted ways."

"What? You've been with the club since the beginning!"

"Yes. But things are different now. People like me have no place in organizations such as this anymore."

"People like you?"

Michl looked at Matthias.

"Matthias, you do know that I'm a Jew, don't you?"

"Yes, but," Matthias stopped himself. He had just remembered the decree from the Third Reich for all sporting organizations to be rid of all of its Jewish employees.

Michl pursed his lips and lowered his head. He took a deep breath, looked up, and then gazed at the stadium. His eyes drank in the sight in front of him. The brownstones, the arches, the flag poles. Each one on their own and together told the story encompassing most of his adult life.

"This palace was my home, Sindi. I will miss Saturdays. I will especially miss watching you play. I will miss watching you out there on the pitch. You made me believe that anything was possible. You made football look so simple. The way you triumphed with such ease. The way you elegantly humiliated your opponents. What I would give to see you do that once more."

Matthias listened. He knew his now-former team boss was not saying this to boost his own ego. He was saying this as a eulogy to better days.

"You brought us glory, Sindi."

Matthias did not know what to say. For a moment he struggled to find the willpower to say something, anything, but he ultimately decided to say nothing. He decided it would be best if he just listened.

"Do you know why soccer matters," Michl asked. Matthias gently shook his head.

"People can explain to anyone different offensive or defensive tactics. The different formations. They can explain the offside rule in simple terms. They can make a list for anyone, off the top of their heads, statistics of how you did in the last match or of the match before that. They have memorized how well you did against this team or that team. They know all these things because you, Sindi, you, and your team, you represent them in a way their government never will. Do you know why?"

Michl tapped his fist into his own chest over and over. He looked into Matthias's eyes deeply and intently.

"Because you make people feel! Everyone who sees you play this game, they work all day, work all day for what? To earn a paycheck to pay someone who works at a bank so they can sleep in a house. That's it. But they come here so they can live! You make them feel alive! You give them something to live for! The Mayor? The Chancellor? The Fuhrer? All they represent is what people read in the newspapers. They don't give anyone a reason to get out of bed in the morning. You do."

Michl stretched out his arm and pointed at the stadium.

"Inside the walls of this building, there's a green rectangle. And inside that rectangle, the people see their true representatives."

Michl took his hand and pressed his finger into Matthias's chest.

"You wear their team's crest over your heart, Matthias. You mean more to them than their individual lives. You represent to them a community of men bound by passion. Bound by a shared sense of fraternity breathing life into their souls."

Michl let out a deep sigh through his nose and frowned. He nodded gently and softly patted Matthias's shoulder.

"I should be getting home, my friend. I hope we will see each other again."

Michl started to walk away.

"Herr Doctor," Matthias said. Michl stopped and turned around to look at the football star he helped create.

"They may say that you can never be part of this organization again," Matthias said. "But you will always be a part of it. You will always be my friend."

Michl smiled and tipped his hat before walking towards his home. Matthias had no idea what his friend and mentor would do next, but he prayed for his safety.

He turned his head and looked at the stadium. He followed the lines created by the edges of the cement blocks up to the apex where the flag poles were lining the perimeter. The tallest one, directly above the main entrance, used to fly the flag of Austria. But now, it flew the flag of Nazi Germany. As Matthias looked at the black swastika in the white circle surrounded by bright blood red, he knew he had to play.

With each step he took, with every swastika he passed, Matthias's feelings of determination hardened.

He kept thinking about what Michl and Heinrich told him. He had a role not only on the field but also off the field and both meant he had a responsibility to play. He finally began to appreciate his celebrity. He finally was beginning to understand why people looked up to him. At first, he thought it was because of his playing ability. Now, though, he saw that it was because of what he stood for. The people of Austria loved him as a man and a symbol of who they were. Whether he liked it or not, he had a voice.

Lost in thought while he walked home, he turned the corner and was quickly brought back to reality. Two elderly Hasidic men were on the other side of the street. They reminded him of the men he had seen when he was a child. Unlike those men, though, these men had their heads down and their arms were up, shielding their faces from the trash that people on the street were throwing at them.

"Hey, Jew!" one young man following them shouted. "Jew! I'm talking to you!"

The pair were trying to ignore them. They began to quicken their pace. That same young man ran up to them and knocked one of their top hats off, exposing his soft balding head. As the Jewish man spun around to catch his hat before it hit the ground, a clenched fist slammed into his face.

The Jewish man fell to the ground. A puddle of blood spread around his wrinkled face. As the young men tackled the other Hasid, fists and feet pummeled them both with increasing fervor.

Matthias ran over to help. He grabbed one of the young men and pulled him off his victim.

"They've had enough!" Matthias shouted, trying to help.

The other men stopped the assault, looked at Matthias, and chuckled. They obviously recognized him.

"Helping a Jew, are you, Paper Man?"

"They've had enough."

The young man looked at the men lying pathetically on the floor, their eyes frantically begging for mercy. He spat on them as he backed away.

"Welcome to Germany!" he taunted one last time before walking away.

As they left, Matthias picked up the top hat. Both men, still reeling, began to sit up. Matthias tried to help them up. He handed the top hat to the one who had it knocked off. The old man dusted off the hat and placed it atop his head. He spat out the blood and felt around his head for the bruise.

"Would you like me to call an ambulance?" Matthias asked.

"I just want to go home," the man responded. Matthias' offer to call for medical assistance would have been futile though as in Hitler's Germany, ambulances were forbidden to rescue Jews. The man struggled to get to his feet, Matthias tried to help him up. "No! You don't want to be in any more trouble than you already are!"

A feeling of helplessness swept over Matthias. He

stepped back and watched the two men struggle to regain their balance. They straightened their jackets and began to walk away from the scene. Matthias stood there, watching them walk away. His jaw hung open slightly. He did not recognize his home anymore. Everything that was happening seemed so foreign and unlike any world, he had ever seen. Earlier, he had to stop young Nazis from assaulting a young girl. Now, he had to stop young Nazis from beating two elderly men to death. What more could he do before the eyes of the evil from the north fixated on more innocent people or on him?

He lowered his head. As he turned around to start heading back home, he felt a lump form in his throat. He longed for the days that Michl spoke of so glowingly. The glory days of when he was a champion. When thousands of people would sing songs for him after he scored the winning goal. The days when his only concern was scoring that winning goal.

As he tried to keep himself from crying, he allowed his mind to wander. He remembered the times he and his friends would fish and camp in the Wachau Valley. He could still smell the freshness in the air he breathed and hear the laughter he and his friends shared. He did not really know the first thing about fishing. He thought that all he had to do was put a worm on a hook that was attached to a string on a pole, then wait for a fish to bite.

The last time he went there was the last time he did not catch any fish.

He was fumbling with his line when an old man named Franz, who was fishing nearby, came over to help him.

"The fish aren't biting because they don't like you," Franz jokingly said to Matthias.

"How can I get them to like me?" Matthias thought Franz was a bit crazy, but he still humored him.

"You need to learn patience. Without it, you won't be able to take the fish home. Sometimes you have to fool the fish. You need to make it think that you aren't hungry. You need to draw it in. Let a few of its friends go. They all know the rules. They know at least one of their school won't be around for lunch. Just be patient, relax your grip, then when the moment is right..."

That time, Franz helped Matthias catch a rainbow trout. It was the first time since he started going on fishing trips that the young footballer did not go home empty-handed and he never went home without a fish after that.

Those memories stayed with him as he walked through the front door of his apartment. This comforting nostalgia quickly vanished as soon as he saw his fiancee, Camila Castagnola. She was sitting on the couch. Her body language spoke volumes. She was impatient and tired of waiting for his return. Her brown hair was normally long and flowing but it was now tied tight in a bun. Her beautiful face was in a pout and her eyes were holding back a scream. Her nostrils flared. In her mind, she was questioning every life decision that brought her to this moment. Why did she give up her modeling career for him? Why did she decide to move out of Italy to Austria? Why did she choose to marry an athlete more in love with the game than with her?

"You're late," was her terse and short greeting.

"I ran into Doctor Michl on my way back," he replied.

Camilla's head turned as if she were a shark that had just spotted its prey. She did not get off the couch. Tension filled the room and her silence was palpable. He knew, instinctively, that he could not just say what he wanted to without her exploding at him in anger. He was trying to choose his words carefully. He consciously slowed down his breath as he carefully hung up his American jacket and Fedora on the hanger by the door.

Camilla was anxious about the outcome of the meeting, even though she knew, deep down, she knew that he would agree to play. There was no way he would ever hang up his boots for good. Even if he somehow lost the use of his legs, he would still figure out how to take part in a pick-up game at the park. But, they had also planned on marrying that spring at her family's church in Italy. If he was going to play in this game, he would have to focus on training for it. So, they would have to delay their plans.

"You're going to play," she asked coldly. "Aren't you?"

"I will," he replied without turning around from the coat rack. He felt the air in the room get heavier.

Camilla remained silent and seated on the couch. She looked at the back of the man she loved and planned on marrying. As she stared, her mind raced. She knew that this was going to be the answer, but now that she heard it, she had trouble finding the words she had rehearsed saying. She wanted to call him selfish. She wanted to call him every name in the book, but she found herself biting her tongue. She was ready to take this next, and important, step in their relationship. But she would have to continue to wait in this engagement chrysalis for a little while longer.

"I had a feeling," she finally said, breaking the silence. "So when will we marry?"

"Maybe in the summer." Matthias walked into the kitchen. The apartment was small and even though the kitchen was in a separate room he could still hear her.

"It will be too hot," she said loudly. Matthias breathed heavily through his nose when he heard her raised voice.

"Then in the winter." Matthias tried not to snap at

her and forced himself to speak in a soft, loving tone. He distracted himself by looking around the kitchen for something to focus on, anything. Then, he looked at the stove quizzically.

"It doesn't matter," she replied dismissively. "We'll just delay the wedding one more year."

Matthias walked back into the main section of the apartment.

"Is the oven still not working?" he asked.

"No. It isn't."

"Is this your way of saying that you want to go out tonight?" He raised his eyebrows hoping to add some levity to the situation and defuse some of the tension.

"Why don't we just leave?" Camilla got up from the couch and walked up to him. She wrapped her arms around his neck. He placed his hands on her hips.

"What are you talking about?"

"We can go to Italy. We can live with my parents until we get our own place."

"Mussolini will probably make me play for Lazio."

"England? America?"

Matthias's head dropped. He let go of his fiancee and freed himself from her embrace. He walked over to the couch and sat down.

"And then what?" he asked. "Canada? Mexico? Just keep running like refugees? I'd rather stay here and live the life I know."

"You'll be branded as a puppet."

"Then let them brand me!" Matthias clenched his fists and screamed silently through his teeth. "No one has a clue about what they've already done. Have you seen what's happening in the streets? People are not people anymore. They act as if no one else matters. People are getting beaten in the street and no one is doing anything! But I have an opportunity. Hopefully, I can remind them of what they had before all this happened."

"You think a football game can make people think supporting Hitler was a mistake?"

"No. I think it will remind them that we aren't like them." Matthias sat back on the couch and ran his fingers through his hair. He breathed deep and stared at the wall. Camilla wrapped her arms around herself and pursed her lips.

"Sindi," she said gently. She slowly walked towards him and kneeled on the floor in front of him. She took his hand in hers and rested her head against his fingers. She did not truly understand what he was talking about. She did not, and could not, truly appreciate the depth of his devotion to his team, nor his overwhelming passion for the game, nor his revulsion for the Anschluss and the current state of politics, nor the pain he was feeling for his aging muscles and joints or the longing he felt for his glory days. She could tell that he had his reasons and that he felt them strongly and passionately. It was clear to her that he did not want to have to explain himself. So she allowed her anger to fade away while she watched his anguish helplessly.

Matthias remained silent and felt the sweetness of her hand and the warmth of her cheek. It comforted him during this uncomfortable time. Feeling her touch gave him confidence. He had his doubts, but he had made his choice. And now, even if it was just mere, feeble words, he had the blessing of the woman he loved.

PART II

"Soccer and the fatherland are always connected and politicians and dictators frequently exploit those links of identity."

—Eduardo Galeano, *Soccer in Sun and Shadow*

The stands of the Praterstadion were empty. The eighteen players on the pitch, Matthias among them, were rhythmically moving through training exercises. On both sides of him were two longtime teammates, Walter Nausch and Karl Sesta. Meanwhile, Coach Heinrich Retschury walked back and forth watching with pride as this team of Austria's finest soccer players prepared for their testimonial match.

"Five more, gentlemen," the coach shouted.

In the grandstands, above the pitch, construction workers were hammering and sawing and drilling. A new section in the stadium was being built and prepared specifically for the government officials who would be attending the game from Berlin.

Heinrich took the whistle that hung around his neck and blew it a few times.

"Alright, boys!" he shouted. "Bring it in and get some water."

The players stopped their exercises and slowly made their way to the sidelines to sip some water. Matthias, with his arms around his chest, looked at the construction above.

"What are they doing?" he asked. He walked slowly as he approached the water table.

"They're creating a throne room," Walter joked.

"Don't make fun," snapped Karl. "They may surprise you."

"What are you talking about?" asked Matthias. He filled his cup with water and took a sip.

"Compared to what we had, how bad could the Nazis really be?" Matthias and Walter both looked at Karl curiously. Walter's eyes widened and his back stiffened. Matthias stared at Karl. They were both taken aback by what their teammate just said. "Schuschnigg was weak and corrupt. He could barely hold this country together. The homelessness, the poverty, it was getting to be too much. The Nazis may not be perfect, but they can't be any worse than what we had before."

Matthias hesitated before taking another sip of water. As he brought his cup to his lips, he not only swallowed water. He also swallowed the urge to punch his friend in the face. He forced himself not to say anything and potentially destroy the delicate fabric that is a National Team representing a nation that no longer existed. This team was made up of players from not only Vienna but all of Austria and they each viewed the current political climate differently. Matthias knew that if he dared speak his mind, which was obviously different from Karl's, he could possibly cause not only a fight but also irreparable damage to the team.

From the corner of his eye, Matthias saw a well-dressed man with an entourage behind him walk onto the field. Heinrich approached the man and the two of them shook hands.

"Who's that?" Matthias wondered allowed.

"Hans von Tschammer und Osten," Karl replied.

"Who?" Walter inquired.

"He's the head of sport for the Reich," Karl answered.

The three players refilled their cups of water. Matthias looked at his coach and the Reich official out of the corner of his eye. He watched as the pair walked slowly towards the team. As they got closer, the group of players all became quiet.

"Gentlemen, Heinrich said. "Please gather around. We have a special guest from Berlin. Hans von Tschammer und Osten, the head of the Bureau of Sport, wishes to say a few words."

"Danke," the official replied. The team looked at him, some with interest. Others, like Matthias, with skepticism and cynicism.

"This match will be one for the ages, for history. We will be celebrating, with this match, the joining together of two peoples separated by an arbitrary and artificial boundary. We were two nations who are now one! We were two peoples, but we have always been one and finally, thanks to the bravery and courage of our Fuhrer, Adolf Hitler, this long division is now ended. Millennia ago, we were separated by Jews who tried to pollute the purity of our Aryan blood and finally, we are correcting this evil. Today, we are united! We are one! We have the Fuhrer to thank for this and this match will celebrate our most glorious Anschluss! No longer are we Germans and Austrians. We are now equals!"

Some of the players clapped at these seemingly encouraging words. As they did, an oversized Nazi flag was being hoisted up on one of the flag poles. The red flag with the black crooked cross nearly blocked out the setting sun as it unfurled in the sky.

"Equals?" Matthias muttered to himself as he clapped with his team, a begrudging attempt to keep up appearances.

March 15, 1938

A giant parade had been staged. German flags flew from nearly every lamppost up and down the streets of Vienna. Austria, now Osterreich, was welcoming their new leader back to the land of his birth with great fanfare and excitement.

It was literally Hitler's homecoming.

The streets of the city known as the Pearl of the Reich were packed with onlookers as German troops rode in triumph and pride as if they had just won a war against the most formidable of enemies. The Austrians clapped and cheered and held their right arms up in the familiar Nazi-salute welcoming the Germans.

At the end of the military caravan, more than a hundred thousand people gathered in the Heldenplatz, the square in front of the Hofburg--a palace which was once the home of the royal family of Austria-Hungary, the Hapsburgs. Nazi flags and banners were draped over the pillars of the building. Rising above the crowd, in the center of the square, stood a statue commemorating Archduke Karl Ludwig Joseph Maria, who ruled Austria-Hungary for most of the 19th Century, and grandfather to the last emperor, Charles I, who was removed from power following the conclusion of World War I.

"We want to hear our Fuhrer! We want to hear our Fuhrer!" the crowd chanted in unison.

Hitler appeared on the balcony of the Hofburg. The roar from the crowd was overwhelming. The impassioned ovation lasted for minutes and minutes more. But the crowd remained enthralled. Many raised their arms as tears of joy welled up in their eyes. These onlookers were burning with enthusiasm. They not only saw him as merely their political leader but also as their savior. The mustached pretender walked with a simple and modest gate, back and forth across the balcony, like a proud soldier conspicuously trying to remain humble, as he saluted them back. Finally, after a few moments of receiving their accolades, he stood in front of the microphone.

"Germans! Men and women!" he said to the crowd. "Within a few short days, a radical change has taken place in the German Volkgeinshaft, whose dimensions we might see today, yet whose significance can only be fully appreciated by coming generations."

The crowd listened to him, hanging on his every word. It was almost as if they were hypnotized by his larger than life character, despite his small frame and ordinary-looking appearance. As he began his speech, he spoke slowly and deliberately at first, making sure that he was emphasizing every syllable.

"In the past few years, the rulers of the regime which has now been banished often spoke of the special 'mission' which, in their eyes, this country was destined to fulfill. A leader of the legitimists outlined it quite accurately in a memorandum. Accordingly, the so-called self-sufficiency of this Land Austria, founded in the peace treaties and the function of preventing the formation of a genuinely great German Reich and hence block the path of the German Volk to the future!"

The crowd booed. Hitler, knowing that he had the audience in the palm of his hand, began to speak more excitedly and with sharp venom in his breath. He knew that many of the Austrians, as well as the Germans, were angry about the Treaty of Versailles which ended the First World War. He knew they felt equally as humiliated as the Germans by the terms of the agreement. Hitler used this anger and discontent as fuel to drive his imperialistic ambitions for world domination.

"I hereby declare for this land, its new mission! It corresponds to the precept which once summoned the German settlers of Osterreich to come here. The oldest of men of Osterreich shall from now on constitute the youngest bulwark of the German nation and hence, of the German Reich!"

The crowd cheered loudly and proudly for their new leader. Many raised their arms to salute him while shouting "Seig Heil!"

He continued: "As leader and chancellor of the German nation and Reich I announce to German history now the entry of my homeland into the German Reich"

Hitler then walked to the rear of the balcony and signed the agreement which formally unified Austria and Germany as one nation.

Sitting silently listening to the events on the radio was Matthias Sindelar. He was sitting in his living room, next to Camilla. Once it was announced that the treaty was signed, he stood and walked over to the radio and turned it off. He stared at the wall while he listened to the crowd's cheers come in through the windows. His eyes darted back and forth while he listened to the adulation which was beginning to sound more and more like an alarum bell for a doomed generation.

The paint on the windows was still fresh. Leopold Simon Drill stared at it from inside the coffee shop he owned, the Cafe Annahof. It was popular among the neighborhood locals until the German takeover of his nation. Now, as the yellow paint forming a ragged Star of David dripped down, Leopold stared, with a feeling of helplessness and fear, at the word right below it.

"JUDEN"

The word graffitied in an angry scrawl in yellow paint was drying on the window of his coffee shop. He was trying to remain strong and hold back his tears but it was impossible. As his focus shifted from the graffiti to the Nazi banner that hung from a lamp post across from his business, a single tear dragged itself down his cheek.

The neighborhood surrounding his coffee shop had

always been one of the most integrated of all of Vienna. The area was known as Favoriten. Members of different ethnic groups and religious backgrounds were living in relative harmony together. It was not uncommon to find storefronts with signage in Arabic, Hebrew, or Yiddish alongside German next to each other throughout the streets of the district.

But now, the neighborhood felt cold and unwelcoming. Stores were smeared with graffiti left by the Gestapo and their sympathizers. Residents were constantly harassed by people who thought it was funny to taunt them. A mere few weeks prior, the minority groups of Favoriten might have been able to walk down the road in relative anonymity. But now, it was as if a target had been painted on their backs—or on their foreheads.

Leopold saw many of his friends leave Austria for France or England or America when they sensed a turning of the tide in the culture and in the government. He and his family could have fled with them but he chose not to emigrate. He chose to stay and remain steadfast. He grew up hearing tales about Napoleon's invasion of Austria a century before and the torment his countrymen experienced at the hands of the French. He considered himself an Austrian patriot.

Whenever Hitler and the other Nazis would spout rhetoric about his brand of nationalism, or anything anti-

Semitic, he thought to himself it was mere bombast and hyperbole. Once Hitler seized power in their neighbor to the north and started expressing what seemed like outlandish threats about annexing Austria, many members of the Jewish community and those who opposed Hitler felt confident that the international community would surely find a way to stop it from happening. They were wrong.

Those who stayed, like Leopold, instead of fleeing the inevitable horrors of the Nazis saw their entire world crumble. Their possessions, heirlooms, life-savings, homes, and more were destroyed or confiscated and became the property of the Reich. Leopold saw his friends, his loved ones, his business associates, his acquaintances maimed, humiliated, and some were even killed in the streets.

As he stared out the window, watching the paint dry ever so slowly on the glass, his mind wandered. His beard might be gray, and the wrinkles around his eyes might be growing, but memories of his childhood came to him and he forgot about his age. Playing football on the field next to the riverbank with his friends. The feeling of freedom he had as he ran and kicked the ball. Bumping into his friends as they all fought for position. He would sometimes pretend to be sick on Saturday mornings so he wouldn't have to go to Shabbat services and instead play football with his friends. That lightning strike of electricity that ran through his body as he kicked the ball as hard as he could, watched it bounce past the goalie and into the goalmouth was life-giving.

Suddenly, the door to his coffee shop opened, ringing the entrance bell, and Leopold was jolted back to the present day. His eyes readjusted as he focused on the man entering his coffee shop. It was Matthias.

"Gutentag."

"Gutentag," Leopold replied, taking his circular-shaped glasses off his face and wiping the lenses clean with a piece of the white shirt he was wearing.

Matthias sat down at the bar. Leopold looked at the celebrity with reverence and curiosity. It was obvious that he recognized who was in his presence, Leopold was trying very hard to hide his excitement about meeting the man who he idolized. He had seen Matthias play for Wien and for Austria many many times. Like all his fellow countrymen, Matthias was one of his favorite athletes. But Leopold was confused.

"Coffee?" he asked the football star. It was not the question he really wanted to ask though. What he really wanted to ask Matthias was, "of all the cafes in all of Vienna, what is Matthias Sindelar doing in mine?"

"Macchiato," Matthias responded. "Doppio, bitte."

Leopold smiled and took a small cup and saucer from the cupboard. He placed them next to the espresso maker and began to prepare the drink for his distinguished customer.

"Is business going well?" Matthias asked, trying to make casual conversation. Both men were conscientiously ignoring the angry graffiti on the window and all that it implied.

"These days?" Leopold turned around to place the coffee on the bar. Matthias smiled in gratitude. He kept his gaze downward as he quietly watched the white foaming bubbles burst one by one. "These days, things are much more difficult than they used to be."

Matthias turned his head and looked around the shop. Matthias slid off his seat and walked over to one of the other tables. He was drawn to it because of the design carved into the sides. The interlacing bands met to form a Hebrew word, "chai" on the corners. A small, half squared letter next to a larger letter, comprised of a small vertical line underneath a larger half square.

"It means 'life,'" Leopold said softly.

"It's Jewish?"

Leopold looked at Matthias with a bit of hesitation. He was about to correct him to say "Hebrew," but instead he stopped himself. He was not sure how to respond. Matthias saw his face and gave him a reassuring smile.

"It's beautiful," Matthias said.

"My grandfather made it."

Matthias ran his fingers over the engraving. He could almost feel the passion of the man who designed this artwork coming through the wood.

"I've been meaning to replace all of the furniture, but I just can't bear the thought of parting with these."

"How much do you want for them?"

"Excuse me?"

"Name your price."

"For the table?"

"And the chairs."

Leopold ran his fingers over his beard and raised his eyebrows.

"Twenty Marks?" He hoped that he didn't ask for too much.

Matthias reached into his pocket and took out his large black leather wallet. He pulled out two twenty Mark bills. He handed them to Leopold who looked at him confused.

"This is too much," he said.

"No," Matthias replied. "You're giving me quite a deal."

Leopold looked at the bills in his hand and then back up at a smiling Matthias. His mouth searched for the words to say. The smile he saw on his face disarmed him.

"Thank you for your kindness," he finally said.

Matthias put his arms around the table and tried to

pick it up.

"It's quite heavy. Please, can you help me carry it to the back and I'll come back for it later with my car."

Leopold cracked a smile. He approached Matthias and placed his fingertips underneath the table. As he stiffened his grip to lift it up, the bell above the door jangled. Two men entered. They stood silently as the door closed behind them. The cafe was filled only with the fading sound of the entrance bell. Leopold turned and as soon as he saw their full-length coats, he knew who they were. They were Gestapo and they only had one purpose for visiting this particular cafe.

"Leopold Drill?" one of them barked.

Matthias shifted his gaze to Leopold.

"Yes," the cafe owner said sheepishly, clearly intimidated by the Nazi-goons before him.

"Drill. Is that Polish?"

Leopold's hands shook almost uncontrollably. The Gestapo chuckled at each other. The tension in the room grew to the point where it could be tasted. Nervously, and in an attempt to hide his fear, Leopold held his hands in front of him and ran his fingertips over his fingernails.

"My family came here many generations ago."

"An Ashkenazi Jew." The two Gestapo pulled out their notebooks and began writing. One of them pointed his pen at Matthias. "What is your name?"

"I am Matthias Sindelar." He tried to hide his nervousness.

"Ah. I thought I recognized you when I saw you entering this fine establishment," the Gestapo said with an obvious tinge of sarcasm. "Tell me, what is someone of your stature doing in a Jew owned business?"

"I was thirsty."

"Yes. The stench of the Jew does make one parched." The Gestapo proceeded to write as he started to walk around the cafe. He made sure his heavy boots pounded on the floor as if he were trying to wake the dead. "Herr Sindelar, you usually patronize the Ring Cafe, don't you?"

"I do." The question did not surprise Matthias. He was a regular fixture on the pages of various tabloid newspapers in Vienna. Anyone who even had a passing interest in the gossip around town would know plenty about him, including where he enjoyed getting coffee.

"So, I'm confused. Why would someone of your-- social status forego The Ring and instead get his coffee from a kike?"

Leopold nervously watched this exchange. The Gestapo officer walked up to a picture hanging on the wall. The image was of a bearded man hammering a nail into a plank of wood. It was a small portrait of Leopold's grandfather.

"I heard that this cafe had excellent Sachertorte."

The answer seemed to satisfy the Gestapo.

"Good. Wien's loss will be Rapid's gain," he said referring to the main rival of Matthias's club team, SK Rapid Wien. He looked at the painting inquisitively. "Herr Drill. Your son has been involved in some questionable activities recently."

Simon's eyes grew wide in fear. His son, Robert, took part in an anti-Nazi protest recently and was arrested. He was swiftly taken to Dachau.

"I assume dissident behavior does not run in the family?" the Gestapo asked sternly.

"I believe quite strongly that my son learned his lesson," came the reply.

"Who is this supposed to be in this painting?"

"My grandfather," Leopold said, trying desperately not to allow his voice to crack. He watched nervously as the Gestapo's pen touched the face of his grandfather's portrait. The Nazi's face widened into a ghoulish grin as he pushed the pen into the canvas and ripped through the old man's gentle face, destroying the picture. Leopold watched in horror. His lip quivered.

"It's lovely," the Gestapo said. He enjoyed how much he was intimidating Leopold. He was thriving off of the sadistic joy it brought him.

The pair walked out of the cafe, chuckling with

each other.

Leopold's arms dropped to his sides. The tears he had been holding back now flooded his cheeks. Matthias walked up to him and placed his arm around his shoulder.

"It's alright," he said, not knowing what else to say.

"No, it isn't" Leopold screamed. "We're all going to die. Hitler won't stop until he is ruling over nothing but a graveyard."

PART III

"The history of soccer is a sad voyage from beauty to duty."

—Eduardo Galeano, *Soccer in Sun and Shadow*

The doors to a house of worship never close. The sanctuary is always open to anyone who wishes to enter. Even when it's empty, the memories remain. The walls whisper the prayers of the parishioners of generations past.

There was a strong chill in the air. The grass was covered in the morning's dew. As the sun shone down, a delicate stream of steam rose to create a soft and delicate mist.

The groundskeeper for the Praterstadion, Rudolf, attended to the pitch with special care. He had taken care of this pitch since the club's founding. He mowed the grass regularly and tended to the soil in the off-season. Each week, he drew the white rectangular touchlines, the halfway line, the center spot, the center circle, and the lines indicating the penalty areas. On his aching knees, wrapped thickly in rags to blunt the pain, he brushed his calloused hand over the grass blades, double-checking and triple-checking the length. As he reached his thick fingers towards the ground, the sunlight glinted off his dirty fingernails which were permanently outlined in thin black lines of soil from years of working in the dirt. He could feel, instinctively through the nerves in his fingertips, from years of laborious practice, the slightest dip or spike in the turf that he cared for. If the grass was too long or too short, the ball could behave erratically and affect the outcome of the game. He cared about this pitch the same way a mother cares for her child.

This stadium, this house of worship, was the community's house. If the game that is played on his field is not a good game, he, along with the coach and the players, could be blamed.

The groundsman looked at the empty seats and imagined the sixty thousand people who would soon be in attendance to see the day's match between Germany and Austria. Not a single one of them will know that his name is Rudolf or even care to know his name. However, they will appreciate his work and the care he had given to the pitch although they will not know who was responsible. The work he did filled him with pride each week. For it was he who helped transform the stadium from a sporting ground into a cathedral. Gazing over the pitch, he always smiled.

The day's match was still several hours away. A devout Catholic, Rudolf left the stadium for daily noon mass at St. Stephen's Cathedral. Today, Archbishop Theodor Innitzer was presiding over the service. Rudolf crossed himself and clasped his hands in prayer. Surrounded by the images of the Saints and flying buttresses reaching to Heaven, Rudolf felt a sense of peace in his heart and soul. Each pew was filled with worshippers, row by row, each person prayed, and sought guidance from a loving God. The Archbishop, who allowed the Nazis to fly their flag atop the steeple, stood at the altar to deliver the homily. Standing in the back of the sanctuary were Nazi officials, listening with great interest to today's sermon as they understood how influential the Catholic Church was in Austria.

"In nomine patri et fili spiritus sancti," he began. "May this day and every day fill us with peace in our Lord and Savior Jesus Christ. May His blessings and love forever be upon us. May He also bless the athletes making up the national teams of Austria and Germany, for they will be honoring the unity of our two peoples with their valiant efforts in today's match celebrating the Anschluss. Football is a magical sport. Each match is a historical moment. The majesty of the sport has the ability to unite people from all over the globe, from all walks of life. For ninety minutes, we are all together as one. The game gives us the ability to believe that absolutely anything is possible. The majesty of our savior's resurrection is on the pitch and in the hearts of the players. Millenia ago, the Emperors of Rome used the games to distract the populous from the failures of their government. But today, the Fuhrer is using the games as an example of our heritage's true greatness."

He knew, deep down, he was not telling the truth. He knew he was saying what he had to say to keep himself and his parishioners alive. Rudolf crossed himself as he joined the congregation in a hushed, "Amen."

The first people to arrive for the match were the newsreel reporters. They set about carefully setting up their camera equipment in the designated areas. They especially wanted to make sure that they had enough room to film the entirety of the field without being blinded by the midday sun.

The next people to arrive were the teams. Dressed in warm-up gear and sweat-clothes, they began running up and down the field. They did stretches. They kicked the ball back and forth to one another. They got used to the feeling of the freshly cut grass on their feet. Each stadium is slightly different from the next, each pitch has its own personality. The soil beneath the grass absorbs, in a spiritual sense, the emotions of the cheering fans and the blood, sweat, and tears of the players. It creates an aura that can not be described, only felt, and understood when witnessed in person. No two soccer pitches are truly identical. They may look exactly the same, but they do not feel truly alike. The rules of the game might be the same across the world, but the ball behaves differently depending upon where it is played.

Slowly, the fans began to make their way to the stadium and find their seats. Once the stadium was mostly full, Hitler and his partei colleagues sat high in the stands above the field in their reserved section. Underneath, the dressing room was crowded with the Austrian players getting dressed in their game kits. The Nazis had provided the team with special jerseys just for this game. The shirts had a new crest, representing Nazi-controlled Osterreich. They were red and bore no connection to any of the traditions or the culture of Austria at all. To the Reich, it made no sense to permit the team to wear their traditional black jerseys with the Austrian crest over each player's heart. After all, Austria had ceased to exist for a few weeks now. It was now known as Osterreich, a region of Germany.

Matthias sat in front of his locker, shirtless, and he rubbed his legs, trying to loosen and massage his muscles. After a moment, he stopped, feeling distracted. He rested his elbows on his knees and clasped his hands as he focused on his breathing. His mind wandered. He was unable to focus on any one thing. He thought about Camilla. He thought about the game. He thought about Leopold. He thought about his nation. He looked at the stool next to him. Sitting on it was his Nazi assigned shirt. He stared at it. He reached over, took hold of it, and looked at the crest. It had the familiar Austrian eagle but at its feet was a swastika. He looked around the room and saw many of his teammates wearing the red jersey. He suddenly felt uncomfortable.

"Wait," Matthias said. "Gentlemen, this isn't right."

The players looked at Matthias. Some of them were confused by his interruption, others were expecting him to give something of a pep talk.

"We should not be wearing this kit. It isn't proper."

"Matthias, what are you talking about?" Karl asked. "This is what we were assigned."

"We are Austrians until the referee blows the final whistle. After that, we can be Osterreich or whatever they want to call us. But when we step out onto the pitch, we need to let them know who they are playing against. They are playing against the Austrian National Team. Das Wunderteam! The team that could not be defeated. The team that caused Scotland to quiver in their boots. The team that was so formidable, Mussolini had to pay off the referees to make sure Italy beat us. That is who the master race is playing today!"

Matthias reached into his locker and pulled out his all-black jersey. He held it up over his head in a proud and defiant grip. The solid-black jersey loomed high, monumental as an obelisk on display by this team's captain. The players gazed at it and Matthias could feel the mood in the room change. The players were starting to understand that this was not just an exhibition match. This game was a statement.

"This is what we should wear today."

Matthias put the black jersey on. He stood proudly and looked at the other players. After a moment of hesitation, Karl took off his red jersey and returned to his locker. Then Walter. Then every other member of the team. They all pulled off their shirts and reached into their lockers to put on the black jersey representing the nation of their birth.

"Never forget," Matthias said while pointing at the Austrian crest that was positioned over his heart. The crowned eagle. In one of its claws, a hammer, in the other a sickle. Over its chest, the colors of Austria, red and white. "No matter what flag waves over our heads, our crowned eagle will always fly free in our hearts. This is our nation, bound together by all of us. We are--today--and every day, the representatives of this, our nation. Some of you will play for Germany one day. But you will still be Austrians when you are playing next to your new teammates.

Always remember, gentlemen, we are Austria."

Matthias put his hand out in front of him. The team put their hands in, forming a bonded circle. Hand over hand, showing solidarity with the team. Some teammates empathized with the Nazis, even voted in favor of the Anschluss. But now, at this moment, they were firmly behind their captain.

"Indivisibiter ac inseparabiliter!"

"Indivisibiter ac inseparabiliter!" Together the team repeated the slogan of the Austrian National Team. Indivisible and inseparable.

The entire team started clapping while slapping each other's backs. They were reinvigorated, ready, and excited. The game was about to begin.

In the tunnel near the dressing rooms, the two teams lined up ready to march onto the pitch. The Germans, with black swastikas emblazoned across their chests on dazzlingly white uniforms, lined up beside the Austrians. Several Germans looked in astonishment at their Austrian opponents. They obviously were expecting to see them in red, not black.

Matthias kept his eyes focused ahead of him. He completely ignored the Germans.

A small orchestra near the field began to play the

opening music, the anthem of Nazi Germany, "Horst-Wessel-Lied." The Wagner-inspired tune filled the packed stadium. The teams began to walk out onto the pitch. Every one of the thousands in the stands raised his right arm in unified salute while they sang the lyrics of the anthem honoring their new leader and their new nation. That leader, Adolf Hitler, who was in attendance, stood with his right hand flung over his right shoulder and nodded his approval.

Matthias noticed, instantly, how different the stadium looked and felt from any other time he had played there. There were now banners and flags honoring the Nazis everywhere he looked. Draped on both sides of the section where Hitler was seated were banners with the German Eagle. A giant swastika looked down on the field like the Eye of Horus. So intimidating was the black cross of hate, Matthias suddenly lost his confidence, something that had not happened to him before a game since he was a child.

"This is a rally," he thought. "Not a game."

Matthias, walking with his teammates, could hear his heart pounding despite the thunderous singing of the capacity crowd. He focused on his breathing to try and calm his heart. He knew this was going to be his last game. He stood stoically with all of the other players at the center circle. The three referees stood between the two teams. All the players, Austrians and Germans, raised their right arms in unison to salute Hitler while the song finished. The Germans and some of the Austrians saluted enthusiastically and proudly. There were a few Austrians though, like Matthias, who saluted merely out of obligation.

The anthem ended. Matthias rubbed his eyebrows and his forehead. He was trying to snap himself out of the distraction of the Nazi rally he found himself in. Then almost out of nowhere as he took his position, he found himself remembering the old man he met once on a fishing trip. Franz.

"You need to learn patience. Without it, you won't be able to take the fish home. Sometimes you have to fool the fish. You need to make it think you aren't hungry. You need to draw it in. Let a few of its friends go. Then, when the moment is right..."

A small smile appeared on his face. He was able to zone out the environment around him. He no longer heard the chanting and the clapping. He no longer noticed the April sun. He no longer noticed the Nazi symbols.

"Sindi!" his coach, Heinrich Retschury, called for him from the side of the field.

Matthias approached the sideline and the skipper placed both of his hands on his shoulders.

"Remember what I told you earlier?"

Matthias did not respond, only stared and listened.

"The game is going to be slow. The game is going to frustrate you. But don't give them too many surprises too early."

Matthias closed his eyes and breathed deep. He nodded slowly.

"You haven't answered my question," Heinrich wanted to make sure Matthias was listening. "Do you remember what I told you in the Ring?"

"I do."

"Good. Just don't score too early. That will just piss them off!"

He slapped Matthias' shoulders and smiled. Matthias ran back to the center circle and prepared for the referee to blow the whistle to start play.

"It's time to fish," Matthias said to himself.

Hitler, from high in the stands, clapped his hands as the ovation ended and sat back down. The rest of his entourage, following his lead, took their seats.

"I will never understand the appeal of this sport," the dictator said to his sports minister, Hans. This was the second soccer match Hitler had ever attended. "It is too slow."

"Mein Fuhrer, I understand," Hans responded. "But the people love it."

Back on the field, the head referee watched Matthias and the German captain, Fritz Szepan, shake hands.

"I don't expect any issues from either of your squads," the referee warned. "Remember, this is an exhibition. This is just a friendly, an exhibition game, and I want to see proper sportsmanship."

"Of course," Matthias responded while staring at Szepan.

Kick-off. The Germans began to play.

The crowd cheered. Their energy was building.

Matthias took his time. He was patient. He allowed the German forwards to enter the Austrian side of the field. He was setting up his play. He was teasing the German pawns by opening up the field to clear the way for his moment to strike.

An Austrian defender intercepted a pass. He passed the ball to Matthias who controlled the ball smoothly, kicking it back and forth between his two feet. He gently guided it around and past the Germans with ease and grace.

Deep into the German side of the field, Matthias found himself with a clear shot, about fifteen yards away. He hesitated before shooting, teasing the goalkeeper.

Swinging his leg, he struck the ball and sent it soaring towards the goal. It bounced off the edge of the goalmouth and then out of bounds.

Clusters of fans stood up in the stands and looked at Matthias in disbelief. A deep moan of anguish rose from their throats. That was not a shot someone like Matthias would normally miss. They had seen him score from farther away and from a more difficult angle dozens of times.

One person in the stands was pleased with what he saw. That person was Hans von Tschammer und Osten. He nodded approvingly.

Throughout the first half, Matthias routinely found himself in scoring position. Each time, he was passed the ball. Each time, he shot the ball just wide and missed. Each time, the crowd gasped. The other players, both Austrian and German, were either without a clear shot on goal or they had their shots blocked. Matthias though, because of his God-given talent as a footballer, was able to find space to shoot. If he did not readily find it, he would create his own space, yet he consistently missed it. Each time he missed, Hans, above in the stands, smiled.

"He could have scored," one fan shouted.

"The score could be five nil right now," another said.

"They got to him," another accused.

As the first half-inched towards the forty-five-minute mark, the score remained as the predetermined tie. When the referee blew the whistle signaling halftime, Matthias rubbed his face with both hands.

As he walked towards the tunnel to the dressing room, Karl and Walter approached him.

"What are you doing? You could have scored!" Walter said.

"It's ok," Matthias said.

"Mind telling us what's going on?" Karl exclaimed. "After that speech, we thought we'd be seeing a different performance from you out here! You're playing like you didn't listen to yourself!"

"Scoring too early would just piss them off. Just be patient. We're a better team and they'll go home knowing it."

He walked away from his teammates and into the dressing room. The stench of sweat filled the tight quarters. He took off his jersey and hung it on a peg in his locker. He then grabbed a wet towel to wrap around his neck and sat on the stool and let his muscles rest.

Coach Heinrich Retschury then entered the room. A lit cigar hung from his lips. He looked at his players. After a moment, he removed the cigar and placed one hand on his belt line.

"Gentlemen," he said. "Why is football the greatest

game on the face of the Earth? Because it brings joy. It is a game of teamwork. Eleven people working together as one unit. It is a game of cunning. It is a game of strength and determination. But why else? It is the greatest game because it brings honor to a community."

When Matthias heard his coach say that, he lowered his head. He felt a sense of conflict because this match was fixed and was more of an exhibition for a political party he despised. He knew he and his teammates were being used as a cog in a wheel of destruction.

"My predecessor, Coach Hugo Meisl, was a great coach to all of you. He taught all of you, and me, everything there is to know about this game. He helped change the game. He is the reason you are called The Wunderteam. When he passed away and the Federation handed the reigns of this team to me, I knew I inherited a great responsibility. You are the greatest team this game will ever know."

He looked around the room and took another puff on his cigar. He then saw Matthias with his head lowered. He assumed Matthias was upset about playing in a match with a predetermined outcome. He was not sure if Matthias was going to score or not.

"Sometimes matches don't end the way we want them to."

Matthias raised his head. His eyebrows arched a

little bit and he took a breath. The two shared a brief smile. Matthias knew this team pep talk was specifically for an audience of one. Heinrich took a moment and walked to the door. He placed his hand on the handle and pushed it open.

"Football is a game of risks. It is a game of chance. And if you do not take a chance if you do not take a risk, then you do not deserve to be on any team in any league. You are the greatest team in the world. Remember that."

He walked out of the dressing room and shut the door behind him.

Matthias stood and threw the towel on the floor. He grabbed his sweat-soaked jersey and pulled it back on.

"Gentlemen," he said to the room. "Let's go out there and show them what we're made of!"

The teams lined up in their positions to start the second half. Before the referee blew the whistle, Matthias looked up to the section where Hitler was seated. He stared at the swastika emblazoned on the arch above the stands. To Matthias it looked like an evil taunt from a laughing bully, it seemed to be screaming at him. The way the Nazi party used the crooked cross was designed to intimidate. He wondered for a moment if he would ever get used to seeing the emblem.

He was jolted back into reality by the referee's whistle.

The roar of the crowd filled the stadium. The rapid kicks to the ball sounded like muffled gunshots. The twenty-two players followed the ball across the pitch in a hypnotic gallup.

Matthias wrestled through several tackles and then passed the ball with a deft kick to an open teammate. The Germans were focussed on Matthias, the best player on the pitch. In the first half, they gave him some leeway which, to their dismay, he exploited and was able to get some clear shots on them. This half, they wanted to shut him down. They wanted to handicap his play and keep the Austrian team from gaining any kind of advantage. The Germans knew who the better team was, it was the Austrians, and the first forty-five minutes proved it. Even in the absence of a scored goal, the Austrians' superior skill with the ball artfully dominated the field of play.

Outside the penalty box, Szepan moved into Matthias with his shoulder and jammed his fist discreetly into his ribs, making sure the referee could not see the sly punch. Matthias fell to the ground, grabbing his chest. The crowd groaned. Outraged, his Austrian teammates screamed and protested, demanding the referee issue a foul and book the German captain.

Szepan stood over Matthias giving him a taunting

smirk and spat at his opponent. He then turned his back and ran after the ball. Getting up, by himself, Matthias turned to look at the German, then ran after Szepan ignoring the pain he felt in his ribs from the punch.

In midfield, the Germans were in control of the ball. The Austrians were on their heels playing defense.

Matthias ran with all his might and slid into Szepan's path. He was able to get the ball out of his opponent's possession. The ball was loose. Matthias got back up and captured the ball. He quickly found space in front of the Germans and made his way towards the goal. A deep roar of anticipation swelled from the stands and filled the stadium.

He was all alone in the midfield with the Germans chasing him. His teammates were all deep in their own half of the field. The German goalkeeper stood just outside the six-yard box with his legs spread and arms extended trying to intimidate the Austrian striker.

Matthias kicked the ball with such force that it flew off the ground in a narrow arc towards the goal. Matthias no longer heard the cheers of the crowd. He no longer heard the foot-stomps from the other players on the field. All Matthias heard was silence. He was focused solely on seeing whether or not the ball would enter the goal.

The crowd held its breath as each fan watched the ball fly over the white line and past the keeper. A moment later, the silence was broken with the swooshing sound of the net catching the ball.

Austria 1 - Germany 0

On the sidelines, Coach Retschury clasped both of his hands into fists and held back his excitement. He desperately tried to hide his excitement from the Nazi officials in attendance. Up in the stands, Hitler placed his hands on his knees. His face became stern and hardened. Hans took a deep breath and looked at Coach Retschury, hoping to get a hint at what was going on with his team.

The crowd erupted in joy. The cheers, the clapping, the jubilation reinvigorated and re-energized Matthias and his teammates. The players' faces were glistening with sweat. Their smiles were beaming and were genuine. Finally, now, the game was real. It was as if a weight had been lifted from Matthias' shoulders. He felt the stress he had been carrying melt away. He had just scored his 27th goal for the National Team and it was this goal that he was most proud of.

Matthias looked at Karl.

"Now that ought to really piss them off," he said.

"No, Sindi," Karl replied. "Now I have to score just to show them that I'm as good as you!"

"If you don't score, I'll kill you!"

The pair laughed and jogged together back to their positions to await the restart of play.

When the teams were ready, the referee blew the whistle to let the Germans kick-off. The crowd was still cheering over the goal that had put the Austrians ahead.

The German players tried to press and break the Austrian defense. They passed the ball back and forth between the midfielders in an attempt to create an opening. But Matthias read their game plan. He went on the attack. Like a shark on the hunt, he targeted the spot where the ball would be and was able to take control of it. Austria was now on the offense.

Anticipating another magical moment from their hero, the crowd cheered even louder than before. Their adulation was like fuel to a flame.

But the Germans managed to close off his advance by crowding the midfield. Matthias looked to his right and saw his teammate Karl Sesta open. He kicked the ball swiftly over to him.

Sesta, from 40 yards out, with no Germans guarding him, with the first touch, kicked the ball directly into the back of the net, scoring the second goal for Austria.

Unable to contain himself, Matthias jumped up and down in sheer, unadulterated jubilation and excitement. He ran across the entirety of the field until he was directly in front of where the Nazi dignitaries were seated. He held one arm out to his side and extended the other across his chest and began to waltz. Dancing with all of Austria as his partner he made the gesture in defiant mockery of his nation's new leaders. As if that was not enough, the crowd began to sing the tune of their beloved "Danube Waltz" guiding Matthias' steps.

"Dah Dah Dah Dah Dah... dah dah, dah-dah," they sang together in glorious union. Fans in the stands wrapped their arms around each other, and danced, bobbing back and forth to the rhythm of the iconic Viennese melody as they sang out with increasing gusto and exaggerated flourishes. The singing and dancing soon gave way to a chant of, "Osterreich! Osterreich!" over and over, louder and louder. It was a symbolic moment. For the crowd was now truly recognizing that their political identity might now be wholly German, but as a people, they were still Austrian.

Hitler crossed his arms over his chest while he watched the Austrian superstar dance and celebrate along with his countrymen. The leader did not allow himself to explode with anger, but he seethed with his mouth clamped shut and his face white, making it clear to everyone around him how displeased he was with this humiliation.

The Austrian coach smiled with his head down, his hands were deep in his pockets. He was hiding his happiness from his superiors. But he did not disapprove of

Matthias so blatantly disobeying orders.

Matthias continued his goal celebration while the rest of the Austrian team gathered around him. They all hugged and slapped each other on the back. For these few moments, they not only felt like the greatest team in the world, more importantly, they knew they were going to win the game.

The crowd was delirious. They did not stop cheering for the remaining twenty minutes of the match. Germany tried to score in an effort to save itself from the humiliation of being shutout but was never able to get the ball into the back of the Austrian net. Finally, as the clock showed 45 minutes had passed, the referee blew the whistle three times, symbolizing the end of the game.

Matthias rose both his arms, clenching his fists, in triumph. He fell to his knees and covered his face with hands. He began to cry. He could hear the cheers from the fans, he could feel their positive energy enveloping him at that very moment. He removed his hands from his face and began to caress the Austrian crest on his jersey. He pulled it up to his face to kiss it. He smiled proudly and joyfully, his tears still rolling down his face.

He looked over to the area in the stands where Camilla was seated. He stood and ran to her. Her arms were stretched open and they hugged each other tightly and strongly. She kissed his cheek.

"You've won more than just this game, Sindi," she said.

Up in the stands where the Nazi dignitaries were seated, it was a different environment entirely. Hitler stood and looked at Hans.

"This is insulting," the dictator said. "This is supposed to be a celebration and this is how I'm treated?"

"Mein Fuhrer," Hans stumbled over his words. "I don't know what to say."

"Football," Hitler said dismissively. "It is such a lowly sport."

Hitler walked past Hans. His entourage followed him out of the stadium. Hans took a deep breath and followed.

Matthias kissed Camilla's hand as he joined his teammates in celebrating the game. It was a victory they were not supposed to have achieved.

The mood in the dressing room changed rather quickly after they showered off. Matthias took the longest to finish. He stood under the water for several extra minutes. As he turned off the water, he noticed the room was silent. He wrapped the towel around his waist and walked towards his dressing area. Suddenly, he felt extremely uncomfortable.

"Come on now, boys," he said joyfully. "We're just going our separate ways, we're not dead!"

He chuckled at his own joke which helped the rest of the players feel at ease. Some of them laughed and the rest smiled. Then, almost at once and out of nowhere, the team began to sing.

"Denn er ist ein lustiger Kerl, denn er ist ein lustiger Kerl!"

As the team was singing "For he's a jolly good fellow," they gathered around Matthias. He tried to join in but it was clear they were singing for him. By the time they reached the end of the song, Matthias had no idea how to show his appreciation. They all clapped and chanted his name a few times.

"You guys are too much!" he said. "Now go win some game with Germany!"

Matthias took hold of his Austrian jersey and looked at the crest once more. He smiled as he ran his fingers over the threads of the emblem. He took a deep breath as he hung it up on the peg of his locker before getting dressed.

His playing days had now officially ended.

PART IV

"Nobody earns a thing from that crazy feeling that for a moment turns a man into a child playing with a balloon."
—Eduardo Galeano, *Soccer in Sun and Shadow*

The office of the German football association was designed to be imposing and ostentatious. Guests could be easily intimidated by the architecture. Known by the acronym DFB (Deutscher Fußball-Bund), the office's high ceilings gave the impression of sweeping grandeur. The dark oak walls were thick with intricately carved pillars and brutal authority.

DFB President, Felix Linnemann, grew uncomfortable during his meeting with Hans van Tschammer und Osten. The match had been held three days prior and Hans wanted answers. Felix was listening to the diatribe with his arms crossed. A lit cigarette sat in the ashtray. The conference table was made out of solid oak. At the head of the room, a large portrait of Adolf Hitler hung on the wall. It encompassed nearly the entirety of the wall.

"Two years ago, in the Berliner Olympics, the Fuhrer was humiliated by the American Negro, Jesse Owens!" Hans shouted. "Then, this week, he is humiliated by one of his own people!"

"I was assured every precaution was in place,"

Felix responded softly.

Hans pounded his fist into the table in frustration. He looked out the window for a moment to collect his thoughts. His face showed a growing sense of anger and frustration that was ready to boil over.

"Is Sindelar a Jew?" Hans snapped.

"Aren't there people in your office who should know that?"

Hans sat back in his chair and crossed his arms. He broadened his shoulders, placed one elbow on the armrest of the chair, and the other on the table. He stared at the wall. Felix picked up his cigarette, held it between his thumb and forefinger, palm facing his lips, and took a drag. Hans turned his head slowly and glared at Felix.

"Don't you have any self-respect? How can you smoke those coffin nails?"

As Felix blew the smoke out of his lungs, he put the cigarette back in the ashtray, smashing the lit end down. Hans looked at Felix as he pulled a letter out of the inside pocket of his jacket. A swastika and the German eagle were printed in the top right corner of the envelope. It was a decree from his sporting office. He rested his elbow on the table and held the letter up, holding it by the corner.

"It is the wish of the other members of my sporting cabinet that there will never be another humiliation like the one we saw on Sunday. At the next World Cup, in France this spring and in the 1940 Olympic Games in Tokyo, Matthias Sindelar will guarantee victory for the Fatherland. Is that understood?"

Felix looked at Hans inquisitively.

"Sindelar? By the time the next Olympics happens he will be 37. He has expressed his desire to retire."

"Our players are the finest on the continent and in the world. They are the most well-conditioned. They are the most well trained and come from the finest Aryan lineage. Uncorrupted blood runs in their veins. Sindelar will be a fine addition to the squad."

"After Sunday's match, and the way you just described how humiliated you all were by his actions, I can't believe you would suggest something so..."

"Brilliant?" Hans said interrupting.

Felix sat back in his chair. Instinctively, he reached into his pocket to pull out his silver cigarette case but stopped himself.

"That wasn't what I was going to say."

"I see no reason why the finest player the continent of Europe has ever produced and will ever produce would not want to represent his nation in these tournaments. He can retire after he wins the World Cup and the Gold Medal in honor of his Fuhrer."

Felix scratched his head. He was aching to light himself another cigarette but he did not want to insult the sports minister.

"It could take some persuasion to convince an athlete who wants to retire not to do so."

Hans placed both of his hands on the table and stood up before leaning over the table.

"Then we will have to persuade him somehow."

Felix sat back in his chair and crossed his arms.

"And how do you suggest persuading him? Threatening him with imprisonment for committing treason? Deportation? Torture? Death?"

"All options are on the table if we are unable to appeal to his sense of patriotism."

Matthias' playing days were now formally behind him. He announced his retirement from international and club play. When he woke up the day after the announcement, he felt like a piece of his self was missing. For the first time in his memory, he woke up without having to train, or to exercise, or to watch his diet. He stared at the shadows from his bedroom's ceiling fan spinning in circles. Round and round. When he would stare at it long enough, it would begin to look like the blades were spinning backward.

He had no idea what to do with himself that day.

Camilla was already awake and in the kitchen.

Still living in Vienna, he repeatedly felt sick because of the sense of helplessness he was feeling. The stench of fear brought on by daily scenes of vile graffiti, smashed windows, bullet holes, and the bullying and public beatings of Jewish people in the city's streets was paralyzing. It was all becoming so common, he felt like there was nothing he could do. His country was now gone and so was the life he knew. He helped a few people who were being harassed, he made thousands of people feel a sense of nationalistic pride with his athletic prowess, but now he was bedridden and feeling pathetic.

He forced himself to get out of bed and take a shower. Camilla, now in the living room, was wearing her robe and reading the newspaper while sipping on a coffee. After a few minutes, Matthias came in, dressed, hair still wet, and walked right past her.

"I'm going to go for a walk," he said.

He grabbed his jacket and his hat and walked out of the apartment. Before Camilla could ask what was the matter, he was already gone.

As he walked out of his apartment building, into a city that was now filled with dreadful scenes, he noticed out of the corner of his eye, a tiny inkling of spring. A small daisy was beginning to bloom inside a crack in the concrete of the building. Its spiky white petals made

Matthias smile and he felt a small gleam of optimism in these dark times. A small, yet hopeful smile began to form on his face. It was a time to begin something truly new.

He decided to walk to the neighborhood of Favoriten and found Leopold's cafe. The yellow graffiti was still on the window.

As he walked through the door, he looked at the back wall. There was now an outline where the painting of Leopold's grandfather used to be.

"You took down the painting?" Matthias asked.

"Yes," Leopold responded. "Macchiato?"

"Please."

Leopold remembered Matthias' previous order and knew immediately to prepare a doppio. The football star sat down at the bar and crossed his arms as his coffee was prepared.

"Listen," Matthias began. "As you know, I love a good cup of coffee. I've spent quite a bit of my money on coffee and I think it's about time I earn some of that money back. That's why I'm interested in going into the coffee shop business."

Leopold smirked as the machine made its familiar noises as it steamed the milk. He poured the macchiato into a cup and carried it over to Matthias.

"Now is an interesting time to be going into business," Leopold replied evenly.

"Why do you say that?"

"Well, the laws of today are extremely strict."

"I'm actually thinking it would be easier to purchase an existing business."

"You'll definitely be able to find yourself a good deal, these days."

"Oh?"

"The Germans are forcing Jewish owned businesses to sell well below market value."

"Are you selling?" Matthias asked while sipping his macchiato.

"I really have no choice. I can't give it back to the bank because they won't take it. Probably because I'm Jewish, but they still want all the money they lent me plus interest. I'm basically being forced to sell it at a loss. But I would implore you not to buy here."

"Why?"

"Because this neighborhood is, well," Leopold paused. "Eyes are everywhere."

Matthias reached into his jacket pocket and pulled out a checkbook. He opened it and began to write a check.

"I would like to purchase your establishment."

Leopold watched Matthias write the check while in stunned, appreciative silence. Matthias signed it and slid it across the counter. The shopkeeper stared at the amount. It was three times what he could have sold it for before the

German takeover.

"I just said that you should not purchase a shop in this area because of the reach of the Nazis."

"I don't care about that. I want this shop."

"But, why?"

"The check will clear," Matthias said ignoring the question. "If your bank refuses to accept the check, please let me know. I will give you cash."

Leopold reached for the check and held it in his hands. He searched for the words to say and he ran his fingertips over its edges, delicately, as if it were a holy object.

"Please tell me why," he implored.

"Because I want to go into the cafe business and I like your location."

Matthias held out his hand. Leopold shook it, his handshaking. He was still stunned by what just happened.

"It was a pleasure doing business with you," Matthias said with a grin on his face.

"I am amazed and grateful."

"I am the one who is grateful."

Matthias smiled as he watched Leopold gaze again at the check. Matthias never told the Jewish shopkeeper the whole truth as to why he wanted to buy the establishment. This transaction was, in a way, another kind of waltz to mock Hitler. He wanted to help him and his family escape the clutches of the Reich. He knew that it would be difficult, but he needed to do what he could do to help, in any way. Matthias, given his celebrity, knew that he had to remain somewhat private. He knew that the Nazis would force Leopold and his family to pay the Reich Flight Tax in order to emigrate. The German government said it instituted this tax to cover any revenue it would lose out because these individuals were emigrating. It was, however, merely a legal ruse to confiscate Jewish property and wealth.

But Leopold did not use the money to flee Hitler. He instead used it to bribe Nazi officials to get his son, Robert, out of the concentration camp. Once he was released, he got his wife and daughter safely to England. Leopold though chose to stay behind.

I can't believe you actually bought this place," Camilla said obviously unhappy with the seemingly rash decision her fiancee had made. She had not seen, nor even heard of the cafe, before he bought it. She was not excited at all. "These walls are dark and uninviting. They need to be painted. The furniture is out of date and looks uncomfortable."

"Your tastes are quite chic, darling."

Matthias stepped behind the bar and began to

prepare to make the espresso.

"You're not Italian. I'm not sure you should try this."

"You never complained about the coffee I make you at home."

"That's because you never called that black water you make espresso."

She sat down and lit a cigarette. She looked around the cafe with resentment on her face. She already hated it.

After a moment, he placed the espresso in front of her. She looked at the espresso and then looked at him, he was smiling. She was not

"Does owning this place make you happy?"

"It does."

She smiled gently and looked back at the espresso. She picked it up and tasted the drink he had just made. "Darling, it's burnt. The water is too hot."

"Too hot? What?"

"You're letting the water get too hot and it's burning the grounds."

"How do I..."

"Here, I'll show you."

Matthias turned around and looked at the machine. He was annoyed. Even though he enjoyed his coffee in the Viennese tradition, bitter and a bit muddy, Camilla introduced him to the Italian tradition of coffee. When he went to cafes and started ordering his macchiatos "doppio," at first waiters would sneer at him. But as the gossip columns spread the word of the Paper Man's Italian fiancee, they slowly understood that he was bringing some of the Mediterranean to Austria.

"Honey, I don't know if our customers will enjoy espresso the Italian way."

"They will because our coffee is actually palatable."

As Camilla came around the bar, the bell over the door rang. The couple turned their heads to see who was entering. It was Felix Linnemann.

"Herr Linnemann," Matthias said, recognizing him. "What a nice surprise."

"Herr Sindelar," the football official replied.

Camilla looked a little confused at the scene as Felix removed his hat and scarf. Matthias smiled as if he knew why the head of the DFB was in his coffee shop.

"This is my fiancee, Camilla Castagnola."

"Fraulein Castagnola, it is a pleasure. I am Felix Linnemann"

"Likewise, Herr Linnemann," she said.

"He is the head of the DFB," Matthias said. "And I think I know why you're here."

"Herr Sindelar, may I sit down?"

Matthias nodded. Felix placed his hat on the bar and sat on a stool.

"Would you like an espresso?" Matthias offered.

"Please."

Matthias turned to prepare the espresso with Camilla's help. Felix looked around the cafe. As Matthias had just purchased it, there was some decorating to be done.

"So you're now in the coffee business I see," Felix said over the sound of the espresso machine.

"I am," Matthias responded. "I think it will be a nice change of pace."

"I'm sure you'll grow to miss the roar of the crowd chanting your name."

"I'm sure. But until then, I'll be making espresso." Matthias placed the cup of espresso in front of Felix.

"Danke."

"And if you're asking me to come out of retirement, the answer is no."

"Herr Sindelar, your nation needs you. We have a World Cup to prepare for and we do not want to see Italy take the trophy again."

Matthias smiled and dropped his head.

"My knees and hips won't allow it. I'm too old."

Even though Matthias was telling the truth, it was not the whole truth. He simply did not want to play football with a swastika over his heart.

"Your nation is asking you to represent all of us, at

least one more time."

"The final game I played was representing my nation."

Linnemann eyed Matthias silently while he took a sip of coffee and placed it back in the saucer. As he continued to hold his gaze on Matthias, he reached into his pocket and pulled out a cigarette, and placed it between his lips. He then pulled out a small matchbook, tore out a match, and lit it. He placed the flame on the tip of the cigarette and took a very long drag as it lit. He breathed the smoke out through his nose while squinting at Matthias through the haze which rose in front of his face.

"That match was nothing more than an exhibition," Felix said. Matthias straightened his shoulders as he listened. To Matthias, it was more than a mere exhibition. It was also an act of defiance. "That said, Herr Sindelar, you played exceptionally well in that match. Even though many people were upset with the result, those same people know that your skills and your clinical expertise for the game will prove useful. We wish to give you the opportunity to show that you did not, shall we say, intentionally cause any kind of humiliation to the ruling party. To the Reich."

"Herr Linnemann, I thank you for your offer, but I cannot accept it. I am officially retired."

Felix took one more long drag on his cigarette

before placing it in a nearby ashtray. He then slowly picked up his espresso and drank it all. He let out a long sigh before placing the empty cup back on the saucer.

"I had a feeling that this was going to be your response. However, I can't say that I'm not disappointed."

Felix reached into his jacket and pulled out his billfold.

"Your money is no good here, Herr Linnemann," Matthias said.

Felix smiled at the insult and put his wallet back in his pocket.

"My colleagues back in Berlin will be especially disappointed to hear this news." Felix stood and reached into his pocket. He then pulled out his business card. He placed it on the counter. "In case you change your mind."

He then picked up his hat and scarf and walked towards the door. He opened it causing the bell to jangle. Before he exited, he stopped and stood in the doorway.

"Herr Sindelar," he said. "I respect your decision. But I cannot speak for everyone else at the DFB or in the Bureau of Sport. I'm sure there are many who will be less than respectful. I hope to hear from you soon letting me know that you've had a change of heart."

Felix gave him a very long sorrowful look. He then exited, allowing the door to close behind him.

Matthias placed both of his hands on the counter

and allowed his weight to rest on his arms.

"They are not going to leave me alone, are they?" he pondered.

Camilla looked at him with sadness in her eyes. She felt truly helpless.

"Let's go back to the apartment," she offered.

"No," he stood up. "I'm going to learn how not to burn coffee! Maybe we can serve Viennese and Italian coffee."

He walked over to the espresso maker and poured water into the chamber. He was oblivious to the two men in the black Mercedes that was parked outside his cafe. They were both staring at him and taking notes about what he was doing. They were the Gestapo.

Viennese nights can be magical, especially when there are few clouds in the sky. The stars glimmer and the moon shines down on the cobblestone streets and the Ottoman-inspired arches on many of the buildings. The quiet spirit of the night can provide a kind of catharsis because it is the time that darkens the past and promises the future. A time that promises a fresh start. A new day, new opportunities, new experiences are all mere hours away.

But nights can also have the opposite effect. They

can produce a sense of dread and uncertainty. That promise of a new day can be horrific.

Matthias stayed awake, lying in bed, staring upward at the darker shadows of the ceiling fan meeting other shadows. He knew that the ceiling was overhead, but he could not see it. Camilla was fast asleep. His thoughts hounded him. Should he not have been so quick to tell Linnemann that he was retired? What horrors will Hitler unleash upon him and his neighbors? Maybe he made a mistake by buying the cafe and he should find another league to play in? Maybe the English league? Maybe in the Scottish league? Maybe in America?

He had been saying that he was too old to continue playing at the international level--which is considered to be the most challenging and intense level of play. But he privately thought that perhaps he could, maybe, ply his trade and squeeze out a year or two at the club level, because playing the game and scoring goals were, after all, what he did best.

"I could dribble past any defense and score against any goalie," he thought to himself. "Yet I choose to run a cafe and I can't make a decent cup of coffee without burning it?!"

The game gave him joy. He felt the pain of realizing that he would never feel that joy again.

He rolled over and stared at a strip of light from a

streetlamp coming through his curtain.

"I wish I never discovered football," he found himself thinking.

He had no memory from his childhood in which a ball was not at his feet. Noisy laughter filled his memories of playing with other friends in his neighborhood or strangers at the park. He was a natural talent. The other children always wanted him on their team.

His father recognized his son's innate gift for the game and his son's natural talent for athleticism. He helped teach the youngster about how to use body language to trick opponents into thinking he would go left when he was really going right. He taught him how to read the game and stay ahead of plays.

He also taught his son the importance of silencing bullies by scoring goals, not by wielding fists.

"Fighting is what soldiers do," he said. "You fight for your nation's honor, not to settle a personal score. If you punch someone, they can punch you back. But at the end of 90 minutes, when the referee blows the final whistle, there's nothing they can do but walk away defeated."

He just did score a goal against the biggest bully he had ever faced, a conquering nation.

"This bully is not walking away, Papa," Matthias thought. "They're going to strike back, I know it! I feel like there's nothing I can do!"

Growing up, Matthias encountered a number of bullies because of his small stature and thin frame. People thought he was weak and feeble. That was of course until they saw him play football.

"People naturally fear what they think is different," Matthias' father told him once when he was consoling him after bullies had been taunting him. "No one should ever insist you change who you are to satisfy their own idea of who you should be. Bullies care more about what other people think about them than what they think about themselves. You don't need someone else to tell you that you are a good man. That's because you are a good man. You are a Sindelar and Sindelars have integrity. Never lose that."

The words of his father and his conscience bounced around in his head as he got out of bed and went into the living room. In the top drawer of his liquor cabinet was a scrapbook. He pulled it out and placed it on the dining table. He then went into the kitchen and pulled out the teapot. He filled it with water and placed it on the stove. He turned it on and then sat down at the table while he waited for the water to boil.

He opened the scrapbook and saw a newspaper clipping of the story about him being sold to Wien. It talked about this young prospect who had the talent to transform the Viennese team into one of the top clubs in all of Europe.

He turned the page.

There was a photo of him with the trophy from his first Austrian Cup. He could not help but smile. He remembered the joy he felt at the time. It was his first major trophy as a professional athlete.

But the happiness was fleeting. His mind kept wandering. He could not help but feel resentment about his present predicament. He pushed the book away and got up from the table. He walked into the kitchen to check on the tea.

The water was not yet boiling.

"I thought she was going to get this thing fixed," he said under his breath.

He pulled the pot off of the burner and saw that it was not ignited, or it had turned off. A ripple of anger traveled through his chest and he smashed the teapot over the stove.

"What's going on?" Camilla shouted. The noise had awakened her. She ran from the bedroom and was standing in the kitchen doorway in her nightgown.

"Go back to bed," he said without turning around.

"What's wrong?"

"Go back to bed!"

"Are you coming too?"

"I'll be there in a bit."

Camilla hesitated for a moment.

"Are you going to tell me what's wrong?"

"I wanted tea and the stove is still not working."

"Is that all that's wrong?"

"What is wrong with you? Go back to bed."

Camilla wished that he would turn around and talk to her. She took a breath and then walked slowly back to the bedroom. Matthias still had not turned around. He continued to stand facing the stove. He looked at the knobs and fiddled with them a bit. He placed the teapot on the counter and grabbed his matchbook. He lit the match and touched it to the pilot light which flared with a brief pop.

He then sat down and looked at the picture of himself holding the trophy. He missed that innocence. He genuinely missed being a star. Being a hero. Being loved by all. Holding his fist in the air after a goal. The roar of the crowd. Hearing thousands of people sing his name. So simple. So glorious.

He sat back in his chair and thought about calling Linnemann in the morning to tell him that he had a change of heart and wanted to accept his offer. Surely, he could put his hatred for the Nazis aside for the ninety minutes it would take to play a soccer game. Afterward, he could ice his aching muscles and joints.

But he knew, in his heart, there was no way he

could wear a soccer uniform with a swastika on it. He felt that it was better that his playing days be officially over.

Matthias looked out the window of his living room. He saw the courtyard below. Hanging from a pillar in front of the old library was the Nazi flag. He looked down and saw a retaining wall made out of red brick. On at least a dozen bricks were swastikas drawn in chalk. The constant and consistent anger he was feeling began to rise through his chest and caused the muscles in his neck and shoulders to tense up, his face flushed hot and red for a moment until he forced his emotions back down and regained control.

The thought about emigrating came back. He could certainly afford the tax he would be forced to pay to get to England or the Americas.

But if he fled, what of the people he left behind? What of the life he wanted for himself in Vienna? He thought that maybe there was something else he could do.

One could be excused for confusing the interior of the Hotel Metropole for an opera house. Built six decades prior, the hotel was the very definition of extravagance with high ceilings, marble Corinthian columns, and a glass-encased dining hall in the inner court.

But arias were not being sung in this building. Nor were any guests staying there willingly. The hotel had been converted into Vienna's headquarters for the Gestapo.

Kriminalobersekretär Jurgen Schrempf had a file full of papers tucked underneath his arm. The Nazi agent was a tall man with his blond hair cut short. He was clean-shaven and his stare was forceful. He was proud to be a member of the Gestapo. He believed strongly in the mission of the Nazi party, to ensure the purity and the glory of the Aryan race. He saw himself as someone who was defending an entire people, by any means necessary.

As he walked through the lobby of the hotel, his footsteps echoing loudly, he passed secretaries and other high ranking Gestapo, until he reached the grand staircase leading to the office of his superior, Kriminalkommissar Max Uhrmann.

As the investigator entered his office suite, Uhrmann's secretary hung up the telephone and stood.

"He is expecting you," she said and motioned to the back room.

He walked past her desk and into his superior's office. It was lit only by a desk lamp. The smoke from Uhrmann's cigarette cast a fine, hazy shadow on his desk. The chief investigator stood at the window and gazed outside.

"Heil Hitler," Schrempf said with his arm raised.

Uhrmann, unenthusiastic, turned, and repeated the greeting. His receding hairline was glistening with tiny beads of sweat in the light from the desk lamp. Schrempf could clearly see that his superior's five o'clock shadow was arriving uncharacteristically early. Uhrmann, a native of the St. Pauli quarter of Hamburg, did not enjoy his assignment in Vienna. He wanted to go back home and wanted to do as little work as possible until he was transferred back to the Northwestern German city. He looked at Schrempf and sat down at his desk.

"What is it, Schrempf?"

"Herr Kriminalkommissar Uhrmann, I have information about the former football star, Matthias Sindelar."

Uhrmann picked up his cigarette, holding it between his thumb and forefinger, placed it between his lips, and took a long drag. He blew the smoke through his nostrils as he removed it from his mouth. He placed it back in the ashtray and then extended his arm, the palm of his hand up.

"Let me see," he said. Schrempf took a step forward and handed him the folder. He opened it and slowly started to read.

"He bought a kike's coffee shop? Why did you bring this to me?"

"He continues to serve Jews, Herr

Kriminalkommissar."

Uhrmann sat back in his chair and grabbed his cigarette. He took another drag from it, burning the end red hot.

"Should I bring him in?" Schrempf asked. Fantasies of arresting the soccer star ran through his head. Locking him in one of the rooms of the converted hotel, tying him to a chair, and beating him during an interrogation excited him. He did not hate Sindelar particularly, but he was anxious to move up the political ranks within the Gestapo and the Nazi party. The arrest of a major celebrity on his record would be a notch on his belt he could truly brag about. Especially this one who had so openly and defiantly mocked the Fuhrer and the Anschluss on the soccer pitch.

"Not yet," Uhrmann turned and looked out the window again. Schrempf was immediately deflated. "These Viennese are prone to rumor and conspiracies. They view Sindelar as something of a god. We can't risk him being viewed as some kind of martyr."

Uhrmann knew of a growing resistance within anti-Nazi circles in and around Vienna. The strongest was an underground network called O5. Despite efforts to quell any kind of rebellion, the resistance grew stronger with each passing week. Jews were getting forged passports to escape Hitler's clutches and political dissidents were receiving help from foreign political allies.

"I will take this up to Herr Huber," Uhrmann said, referring to Franz Josef Huber, head of the Austrian Gestapo. Schrempf nodded, slightly more encouraged. "In the meantime, continue monitoring his cafe. Report back to me of anything else that seems alarming."

Schrempf raised his arm, shouted, "Heil Hiter," enthusiastically and left the room. As the door closed behind him, he wondered if Huber would ever see the file.

I t was early Saturday morning. Mist hung over all of Vienna. The sun was starting to rise and the owls sang their sad song lamenting night's end, letting the world know they would return the next night.

Matthias stepped out of his apartment building and took a deep breath. he still was not used to the idea of waking up on a Saturday morning without having a game to go to in the afternoon. It was a transition he was still trying to come to grips with. He genuinely missed playing.

But his memories of his playing days were quickly swept away by the sounds and smells of a nearby bakery. The aroma of Bavarian pretzels roasting, pastries baking and coffee brewing filled the air. It made Matthias notice that he was hungry. He did not have time to stop for food though because he had a cafe to open.

As he walked, he noticed a pair of men walking

about a half-block behind him. He did his best to give it no mind, but he kept noticing them. He felt their presence at his back as he walked. When he turned a corner, there they were. It was clear that they were following him.

He looked up the road and saw a black Mercedes, the same one that was parked in front of the cafe when Felix Linnemann came to visit. He shook his head as he looked for the key to enter his new cafe. Once he found it, he slipped it slowly into the lock. He felt the grooves of the key move over the tumblers and the bolt. As he turned it, he could feel the resistance pressure between his fingers. It caused the key to feel heavy.

He opened the door and crossed the threshold. He picked up a newspaper which sat by the door before closing it and locking it. He turned on the lights, placed the paper on the cafe bar, and filled a pitcher with water. He poured it into the espresso machine to heat up and began to grind the coffee beans leftover from the day before. Once he had ground enough coffee for the first few customers, he prepared the till and counted out the change.

With Camilla's help, Matthias perfected the process of brewing the perfect cup of espresso. At her insistence, she took over decorating the establishment. On the walls, she hung pictures and posts of his sporting triumphs. There were framed newspaper articles about him, his various victories, and his God-given talent. There were posters of ads for products he endorsed, like yogurt and shoes, and snapshots of him and his teammates.

Matthias insisted that she not replace the furniture. He felt there was an unspeakable and indescribable genuineness and authentic feel to the work Leopold's grandfather put into making the tables and chairs. Whenever he looked at the designs, he felt a soft feeling of comfort. Even though he knew that it was now contraband because of the Hebrew lettering adorning it, he did not want to part with them. Having this small homage to the cafe's past, and his nation's past allowed him to feel like he was engaging in another act of defiance that was all his own.

There was a knock on the door. It startled him. Matthias looked up and saw a young girl, about ten years old, holding two wicker baskets. He smiled. She was dropping off pastries for him to sell that day. He bought some of them from her and prepared the treats in a display at the bar. He flipped over the "OPEN" sign on his window.

Almost as soon as he formally opened the cafe's doors to business, the first guests started to arrive. Matthias greeted each one with a smile and a warm welcome. He tried to keep up with the orders for coffee. Two men walked in tentatively. Both wore black wool jackets and had beards trimmed close to their faces.

"Guttentag!" Matthias said to the men.

"Is Leopold still here?" one of them asked tentatively. There was a note of fear in the man's voice. The other man's face drew long with a sense of foreboding, clearly expecting to hear that Leopold had been taken away by the Gestapo.

"I purchased the cafe from him. Please come in, take a seat."

The men were not sure if Matthias was telling the truth but knowing that their friend could possibly be alright comforted them.

As the morning rolled on, there were about twenty-five customers enjoying their breakfasts and coffee. The men who had been following Matthias then walked in and past him at the bar. They walked towards an empty table in the back of the cafe. Their heavy boots tapped the floor loudly with each footfall. Their black overcoats were long and reached down to their ankles. They did not take off their overcoats while they sat down in silence.

Their silent presence not only bothered Matthias, it also bothered the other customers. They were intimidating even though they were not doing anything. Once there was a lull in coffee orders, he walked over to the men.

"Gentlemen," he began. "Would you like to order anything?"

They looked up at him, silently.

"I'm very sorry," Matthias said in an effort to intimidate them. "But if you are not going to order anything, I'm going to need to ask you to leave."

"I'll take a glass of milk," one of them said.

"Milk?" Matthias raised his eyebrows at the odd request. "I'll be right back."

The two men chuckled with each other as they each reached inside their jackets and pulled out notebooks. They both began jotting down some notes. Matthias came back with a glass of milk and placed it on the table.

"Will there be anything else?"

The man who asked for the milk threw five marks in change on the table. The coins jingled on the wood, some of them fell on the floor.

"One question, Herr Sindelar."

"Yes?"

"How many Jews are here right now?"

Matthias took a slight step back but broadened his shoulders. He took a moment as he thought about how to respond.

"I wouldn't know. I just ask them what they would like to drink, not what God they worship."

Matthias walked back to the bar.

Both men shook their heads. The man who ordered the milk took a sip from his glass and then placed it back on the table. He wrote something in his notebook, closed it, and placed it back in his coat's pocket. He motioned to his partner and they stood to leave.

As they passed the bar, they both stopped and looked at Matthias.

"It would be wise for you to be a little more cognizant of the type of clientele you allow in here, Der Papierene."

He deliberately spoke loudly enough for everyone in the cafe to hear him. Upon attracting everyone's attention, they walked out of the cafe. Matthias watched them leave. Once they were outside, he went to the window and watched them cross the street and get into the back of the black Mercedes waiting for them.

In the car were four men, all Gestapo. Seated in the front passenger seat was Jurgen Schrempf.

"What did you learn?" Schrempf asked authoritatively.

"There were no known Jews there," one of the men in the back said. "A few looked like kikes though. Most disturbing, he's certainly indifferent to the idea of serving them. Even insulting me when I asked him about it."

"What did he say?"

"He defiantly said that he won't ask them what God they worship as if being Jewish is just a religion."

"I see," Schrempf said as he grew more frustrated. He wanted to send in his officers and arrest everyone in the cafe, Matthias included. He wanted a clean sweep of Jews and Jewish sympathizers in his city. He wanted to be commended for his service to his country and to his party.

"We should do a sweep," one of the men in the back seat said, basically reading Schrempf's mind. "Let's bring everyone in!"

"We should but we can't yet," Schrempf said begrudgingly. "Believe me, I wish we could. But we have our orders. We can only collect information and evidence. Then when Uhrmann feels like we have enough, then we can bring him in."

The four men sat in the car in silence for a moment. They watched intently as men and women entered and left Matthias' cafe. Then, the driver turned the engine over and the Mercedes drove off.

Sepp Herberger loved football. It was not just a game for him, it was his philosophy of life. He viewed the world through its lens. To Sepp, the game was the epitome of masculine grace, physical discipline, and fraternity. And his devotion to winning through unsurpassed performance on the pitch was his life's work. As head coach for the German National Team, he used this life philosophy to turn the team into a formidable opponent.

Some said he ran the team the same way a drill sergeant would run an army platoon. He did not believe in days off, his players were always preparing for the next match and should be ready to lace up their boots at a moment's notice. His players were instilled with a sense of confidence that was practically unmatched. He did not want them to be intimidated by the other great teams of the day, like rivals Austria or Argentina or England or Uruguay. He would tell his team, that no matter where they played, "the ball is round and the game lasts for ninety minutes." The basic elements of the game were always the same. There was a deep and abiding certainty in this pronouncement. The Germans' muscular and aggressive attack kept fans on edge and opponents on their back heels. The combination was marvelous.

The DFB, following orders from Adolf Hitler, insisted that they needed him to bring in some of the Austrian players to the German National Team for the upcoming World Cup. Sepp had his reservations.

The coach sat at the end of a long table inside the headquarters of the DFB, Felix Linnemann and Hans von Tschammer und Osten were on the other end of the table facing him. They were going through the Austrian roster to figure out who would best fit into the German National Team. Sepp struggled to find the words to politely object to the idea of bringing in the Austrians, but he was left with little choice. Hitler had ordered that half the German team be made up of Austrians. He was convinced that the combined forces would make the team completely unbeatable.

Even though the coach helped turn the German team into a difficult team to beat, he knew that not every player would fit nicely into his system and style of play. Some players flourish under different coaches and different styles, and the Austrians played a very different style of football than the Germans. Where the Germans were very regimented and stuck to their positions using brute force to move the ball up the field, the Austrians were more free, known for swift passes and a free-flowing style of play to score goals. Neither style was necessarily better than the other, they were just different styles of play that worked or did not work for different players. Coach Herberger had serious doubts about being able to coach a player who was so used to playing a style of play that was antithetical to what worked best for him. But the decision was not up to him.

"Not Karl Sesta," Hans said defiantly.

"Why not?" Sepp asked. "He's a key player. I might be able to mold him to our style of play."

Hans and Felix look at each other and had a silent conversation. Unbeknownst to Sepp, the pair decided that because of Sindelar's refusal to play for the Reich, the players with whom he was friendliest would not be invited to join the team for the 1938 World Cup.

"The answer is no," Hans said. "And no to Walter Nausch. Who else is there?"

"Why not Nausch?" Sepp asked.

"His wife is a Jew."

Sepp searched for the words to respond to Hans' reasoning. He began to speak slowly and chose his next words carefully.

"Since Sindelar is retired and he has no interest in coming out of retirement, why not bring along two of the three standouts of the Wunderteam?"

"The answer is no. We'll have to choose other players."

"Gentlemen," Sepp began. "We are stuck in a corner. I do not like the idea of being forced to call in the Austrians but obviously, we have to. Why cripple these efforts further by not bringing in the best players possible? Sesta and Nausch don't play the game the way I like but they are fine players and can adapt. I've seen them adapt and I know I can coach them."

"Choose two other players," Hans said as he got up from the table. After he opened the door he stopped to have one final word. "We will not reward those who take joy in betraying their race! I will not let them spit in my face again."

With that, he slammed the door behind him.

"What is he talking about?" Sepp asked Felix who was urgently reaching for a cigarette.

"Hans hates the smell of cigarettes," Felix said, cigarette already in his mouth. "He is also a stubborn man. That's why he's in charge of the sports bureau."

"I have to coach a team in the World Cup with players who are not suited to the German game! The World Cup! With Sesta and Nausch, we might have a chance. Without them..." Sepp knew he was fighting a losing battle and did not finish his thought.

Felix took an extremely long drag on the cigarette and his exhale seemed to be even longer.

"Sepp, you've been a coach for a really long time. You've done some magical things with the national team. You've got several more wonderful years ahead of you as a coach too. You know as well as anyone that when it comes to coaching, you sometimes have to make some really difficult choices. Right now, you've got to choose a squad. I have an idea about Nausch, I'll talk to Hans about it. But you can't choose Sesta. I don't think I'll be able to get him to change his mind about him. Alright?"

Matthias' and Walter's friendship extended back to their early playing days. They first joined Wien together when they were in their early 20's. When they were not scoring goals and winning games, they were womanizing and dancing and drinking-- activities that slowed down greatly as they got older. Not only did it start to take longer to recover from the night before, Walter got married and Matthias was planning on marrying.

Now, whenever they got together, their significant others joined them and they spent their evening playing cards, smoking cigars, and sharing a beer or two. Their favorite was Gosser. Matthias had two bottles in a brown paper bag in one hand, Camilla's hand was in his other as they walked into Walter's apartment for an evening get-together.

"Why aren't you packed?" Matthias asked as he entered the apartment.

"Packed?" Walter responded.

"For France!"

"Haven't you heard? I was cut," Walter said matter of factly as he sat down at the poker table. Matthias stood in the center of the living room stunned. Camilla clutched her handbag not sure how to react. "Along with Karl. Several others too."

"Cut?" Matthias placed the paper bag on the table and sat next to his friend. Camilla walked into the kitchen and found Walter's wife, Margot, exiting this uncomfortable and difficult conversation. "Both you and Karl? Do you know why?"

"Because of Margot. She's Jewish." Walter reached into the bag and pulled out one of the beer bottles. He placed the bottle between his knees while he grabbed the opener and yanked off the cap. "They told me that I could play in the World Cup and then become manager of Wien after the games if I divorced her. I told them there was no way I would divorce my wife."

Walter poured his beer into a glass and took a sip. For a moment, they sat in uncomfortable silence. Matthias sat back in his chair while his friend's shoulders slouched. Walter lifted his beer and brought it to his lips to take a sip.

"We're going to go to Switzerland," Walter said.

"You're going to flee?"

"We are going to do what we have to do in order to stay together." Walter picked up the deck of cards and began shuffling them, almost nervously, watching the cards slide over one another hypnotically. "Are we going to play some cards or are you just going to try and depress me?"

"Deal up! Five-card draw?"

Walter dealt out five cards to Matthias and also to

himself. As they looked at their cards, Walter glanced at Matthias.

Walter placed two cards down. Matthias placed three. Walter dealt out the replacement cards to his friend. Poker and soccer are two very different games but both have many similarities. Both are games of deception, risk, and luck. In both games, the players are trying to trick and fool the others into thinking that something else is actually going to happen. In soccer, a player is trying to trick a goalie into going to the left when he is planning on shooting the ball to the right. In poker, a player is trying to convince the other players he has a better hand than he actually does. To be an expert soccer player and an expert poker player, one must have confidence, guile, cunning, and a bit of good luck.

Neither Matthias nor Walter were as good at poker as they were at soccer, especially after drinking a few beers and smoking a couple of cigars. But they enjoyed each other's company and playing poker together while their wives socialized. It allowed them a chance to reminisce about their playing days on the pitch, forget about their ages for a little while, and make fanciful plans for vacations they would go on with their ladies to Budapest, or Paris or New York.

"Camilla has talked about wanting to go to America."

"To visit or to move to?"

"Darling," Matthias shouted. After a moment, Camilla stood in the doorway between the bedrooms and the living room holding a glass of wine. "Darling, do you want to move to America or just visit?"

"Why would anyone want to move to America and leave Vienna?" she said with a smirk on her face. "Do they even play football in America?"

"Yes, but not very well," Matthias said while collecting the cards and shuffling them. His cigar was in the corner of his mouth.

"They call it soccer there," Walter said.

"And in Italy, we call it Calcio," Camilla said before blowing Matthias a kiss and turning back to the bedroom. "Caio!"

"Sindi," Walter said. "Whenever you go to America, make sure you pick me up one of those hats the cowboys wear!"

Matthias laughed and shook his head. He reached into his pocket and pulled out his wallet.

"One more game!" he said enthusiastically as he placed a five-mark bill on the table. He began to deal out the cards and Walter picked up his hand.

"You know, Sindi," Walter began delicately. "There's a question I've been wanting to ask you."

"What's that?"

"Why didn't you tell us that the game was supposed to be a draw?"

Matthias hesitated as he looked at his cards and organized them.

"How do you know that it was supposed to be a draw?"

"It was, wasn't it?"

Matthias placed the cards face down on the table and stared straight ahead.

"I couldn't." Matthias' eyes became unfocused. It was almost as if he were falling into a state of hypnosis.

"What do you mean you couldn't?" Walter was not being accusatory, he merely wanted an answer.

"I was told. Orders."

"From the Nazis?"

Matthias paused for a moment.

"Heinrich," he said softly. "He felt that there would be a concern that it didn't look like we were trying to score, and trying to win, that it wouldn't look real. I believed him."

Walter leaned over the table and placed his hand on his friend's shoulder.

"Sindi, I'm not bothered that the game was supposed to be fixed. Especially since you helped make sure that we won and thumbed your nose at you know who. I'm bothered that you didn't tell us."

Matthias' shoulders dropped and he hung his head. He struggled to find the words to say. Matthias took a deep and heavy sigh.

"I couldn't. Heinrich asked me not to say anything," Matthias' voice trailed as he tried to find the words to explain the situation to Walter. "He explained that the game needed to look real to the spectators and the press. How did you find out?"

"There have been rumors about it."

"What about the rest of the team?"

"Some of the players heard the rumors too. It makes sense though. That first half? You weren't yourself."

Matthias pulled a packet of cigarettes from his pocket. He grabbed one and then placed the small box on the table. He picked up a lighter but did not light it. He merely rubbed his thumb over the edge.

"I'm afraid, Walter. I'm afraid for our world and what we've become. I'm afraid for you, I'm afraid for our neighbors, I'm afraid for my family. I'm afraid to walk down the street. Before the game, I saw two old men being taunted and beaten in the street. I saw a group of men who tried to take advantage of a young girl. All these Nazis walking up and down the street acting like they can do whatever they want like they own the world. I'm afraid. I'm afraid to be in my own home. Walter, I was in an impossible position. These days, what we say is as dangerous as what we don't. The Nazis are ruthless, and I was not going to allow them to get what they wanted. We are not like them. So I did what I did so Austria could win one last time. It was the only way to save our team's honor."

Walter reached out and tried to grasp Matthias' hand but he was still in a daze. So instead, he held his wrist in an attempt to let him know that he was forgiven. Matthias was, at his core, a man of honor and Walter wanted him to know that he knew that and respected it.

PART V

"Some people think football is a matter of life and death. I assure you, it's much more serious than that."

—Bill Shankly

In the summer of 1938, the world's fifteen best national teams came to France to compete for the Jules Rimet Trophy in the third ever World Cup. Sixteen teams were supposed to compete, as decided by a qualification stage held the prior year. But, because of the Anschluss, Austria withdrew from the tournament even though the team qualified. FIFA decided against finding a replacement.

Germany's first match was against Switzerland at Parc des Princes, in Paris. Matthias was listening to the match on his radio at his cafe. About a dozen soccer fans also gathered to listen, eagerly anticipating the outcome.

When striker Willhelm Hahnemann, one of the Austrians playing for Germany opened the scoring in the 8th minute, they cheered wildly. In the twenty-second minute, Swiss player Ernst Lortscher accidentally kicked the ball into his own team's goal giving the opposition another goal, they cheered even louder. It seemed certain that Germany would win the match and advance into the tournament's next round.

But that would be the last goal scored for the

Germans. The Swiss would go on to dominate the rest of the game and score four unanswered goals. The first two goals were met with moaning and groaning from the soccer fans in the cafe. As for the third, they were in disbelief. When Andre Abegglen put in the fourth and final goal of the match, they were devastated. Germany, their new nation, was out of the competition.

After the referee blew the final whistle, Matthias turned the radio off. He felt like he had been punched directly in his gut. He felt a deep sense of sadness for his former teammates. He was concerned for some of them. He knew what it would be like in the dressing room after such a devastating loss. There is resentment. There is anger. There is frustration. The silence can create a thick deafening tension that could be cut with a knife. That new German National team was made up of players who were forced to become teammates. A few months earlier, most of these players were from two different nations playing two different styles of football.

All the players in the dressing room were replaying the entirety of the match in their heads. They were so on edge that any one of them could lose his temper at another teammate for what would ordinarily be nothing at all -- an accidental push at the shoulder upon passing each other in such close quarters, a loud noise, or even someone sighing heavily could set someone off. But of course, the anger was not really meant for their teammate. They were really mad at the outcome of the game, or at themselves for their own performance in the game and some little thing would merely set them off.

Football might be a game of tactics and endurance on the surface, but at its core, it is a game of emotions. It is a game built on passion.

Italy would go on to win the World Cup for the second time after defeating Hungary in the Final.

PART VI

"Whoa to you on Earth and Sea, for the Devil sends the Beast with wrath for he knows his time is short..."

—Revelations 12:12

udolf, the groundskeeper of the Praterstadion, walked into St. Stephen's Cathedral for mass. Before finding his usual place in the pew, he lit a candle and said a prayer for his late mother. He crossed himself, turned around, and entered the sanctuary. At first, he was taken aback because there were about nine thousand people attending church on this day. Usually, the church would see nine thousand people only for Christmas or Easter. It was rare to see this many people for a Saturday evening mass, but it was announced that at this mass, there would be a discussion about the relationship between the Church and the ruling-Nazi Party.

Since the Nazi takeover of Austria, the Catholic Church was treading on the delicate ground with the new oppressive government. The Diocese initially publicly supported the Anschluss, even allowed the Nazi flag to fly over the flag of the Vatican atop the cathedral. But the tide of support was beginning to turn. Many priests and nuns were also arrested for allegedly challenging the state, charged with treason, and sent to concentration camps.

The groundskeeper found a seat in the back next to

a young man barely in his twenties who he did not recognize. Rudolf was encouraged by the number of young people he saw this day. He began praying silently, clutching his rosary beads.

After a few moments, Theodor Innitzer, Archbishop of the Viennese Diocese, stepped to the altar. He looked before his assembled flock and rose his hand to his shoulder. He glanced down at his bible.

"In nomine patri et fili spiritus sancti," he began. Rudolf looked around the packed hall and saw a familiar face a few pews up. It was Matthias. Camilla clung to his arm. Rudolf smiled and then turned his head to listen to the words of the Archbishop. "My friends and family, the youth of Vienna, in the last few months, you have lost everything!"

The nine thousand people in attendance began to stir uncomfortably. Many people leaned to the person next to them and whispered.

"You lost your Catholic youth groups and your Christian unions, but I am sure you will, nevertheless, join with your priests in the great union of the Church. I know that some of you have not approved of the attitude of the Bishops in the past, but you did not, perhaps, fully realize the tremendous responsibility of the Hierarchy. Whatever may come, I know that there is high principled Catholic youth which will not run after empty phrases!"

Many in the audience nodded approvingly.

"The Devil has effectively tricked us. The devil deceived Eve in the Garden of Eden. He tricked Judas into the betrayal of the Messiah and now he is tricking all of us. Therefore, we must stop his trickery and deceitfulness once and for all. We must confess our faith in our Fuhrer, for there is just one Fuhrer: Jesus Christ!"

The fighting words were met with an audible gasp. Many young men jumped to their feet, fists clenched in the air. They were shouting their objections and protestations in a fury of spite.

"SEND HIM TO A CONCENTRATION CAMP!"

"TRAITOR!"

"DOWN WITH THE CLERGY!"

These young men were trying to rile up the crowd against the bishop who stood bravely behind the altar. Almost inspired by the sight of the religious leader, a counter-protest erupted. Many of the faithful stood in defiance and shouted back, "CHRIST IS MY FUHRER!"

The angry words quickly gave way to fists. The cardinal was pleading with his congregation to stop fighting but it was too late. A young priest approached his superior and begged him to leave the cathedral and find someplace safe.

The arguments in the pews spilled out into the streets. People were being punched and shoved. Matthias found himself on the receiving end of a punch as he was trying to get away, hustling Camilla along as he grasped her shoulders. Rudolf grabbed them both and pulled them into an alley behind the church. Both men were gasping for breath as Camilla wept.

"What is going on?" Matthias asked rhetorically.

"Our church just decided that we made a mistake last Spring," Rudolf responded. Matthias rubbed the sweat and blood from his eyes and then looked at the man who pulled them away from the melee.

"Rudolf?" Matthias looked at him inquisitively.

"Herr Sindelar."

"My goodness!" Matthias reached out his hand to shake his friend's. "I wish we could have met each other again under more peaceful circumstances."

"I think we both know that we won't see peace again for quite some time," Rudolf said remorsefully. "Come now, we should get home. Make sure you keep your lady safe."

While the brawl in front of the church went on, the pair ran off to their respective homes. Matthias made a mental note to try and stay in touch with Rudolf. Soon, the police arrived, arresting people indiscriminately. The priests rushed Cardinal Innitzer to the seminary which was a few miles away.

The next day, members of the Hitler Youth broke

into Innitzer's home. They smashed all of his belongings and ripped up his papers and books. During the raid, someone opened up one of his many copies of the Bible to The Gospel of Luke, chapter 2 verse 7. This passage describes the birth of Jesus in a Bethlehem stable after a long journey. The young Nazi threw the holy text on the ground and proceeded to urinate on it.

Matthias woke up the next morning with a bit of a cough and a splitting headache. His head was sore from getting socked the night before. As he got out of bed, he tried not to wake Camilla who obviously was exhausted from the previous day's ordeal. She was so shaken that she cried bitterly while she tried to get herself to fall asleep. He walked into the bathroom and looked in the mirror. There was a small black and blue bruise on his cheek that he hoped would go down soon. He stepped into the shower and began his day.

As he stepped out of the apartment building to go to the cafe, he stopped at a newsstand because the headlines of the tabloids caught his eye.

"ASSASSINATION IN PARIS!"

"HORROR AT EMBASSY!"

"JEW KILLS DIPLOMAT!"

Matthias approached the newsstand and purchased

one of the papers. He looked closely at the front-page story. A German diplomat working at the consulate in Paris, Ernst vom Rath, was assassinated by Herschel Grynszpan, a Polish Jew living in France. As Matthias read further, he learned that investigators believed that the assassin was agitated by the forced deportation of Polish Jews who were living in Germany. Grynszpan's family was amongst the twelve thousand who were forcibly removed from their homes. For a brief moment, Matthias thought of Leopold who had sold him his cafe and how he was hounded by the Gestapo with their sneers of "Polish Jew."

The papers offered little else in regard to the killer's motives. Only saying that the assassin purchased a revolver before going to the German embassy. He asked to speak to an official and was sent to vom Rath's office. Once inside, Grynszpan shot him five times. He gave himself up to the police almost immediately. In his pocket was a postcard addressed to his family. It read, "With God's help. My dear parents, I could not do otherwise, may God forgive me, the heart bleeds when I hear of your tragedy and that of the 12,000 Jews. I must protest so that the whole world hears my protest, and that I will do. Forgive me."

Matthias was having trouble making sense of the killer's motives. All the typical storylines for assassinations seemed to be missing from this one. After all, vom Rath was not the French ambassador to the Reich, he was only a junior official. If this was because of the treatment of the Jews and Grynszpan's family, why would he target someone who is a low ranking embassy official?

He folded and tucked the paper underneath his arm and made his way to the cafe. Once there, the assassination was the only topic of conversation. The faces of his Jewish customers were paralyzed in fear.

"All we can do is pray that no one seeks unreasonable retribution," an older customer said to Matthias.

"I hope you are correct," Matthias replied. "They caught the man who did it, he did not seem to have any accomplices."

"But look at America!" the customer said loudly.

"What do you mean?"

"How many redskins are left in America? They killed almost all of them! They passed laws and made it legal to treat them like dirt. They forced them out of their homes! They were gunned down if they resisted. Beaten! They were hung! It didn't matter! Their only crime was existing. What the Americans were doing was legal in the eyes of their own lawmakers. They forced Indian children to be separated from their parents. The American soldiers ripped mothers and children apart. Those children were put in boarding schools, given new, American names, all in an effort to strip them of anything that made them Indian. They were forced to learn to be a completely different culture. And that is what is going to happen here! Hitler and his disciples will do to us what the Americans did to the Indians!" He paused for a moment to make sure Matthias was listening. "If Hitler is half as kind to us as the Americans were to the Indians, perhaps we'll fare a little better than they did."

Matthias stared at the older man, speechless. The fear and uncertainty were so abrasive in the community, it was almost crippling. Yet, enjoying this mere cup of coffee was a small respite that allowed them, for a few moments at least, to feel like a person in a nation where they were now viewed as subhuman.

"All we can do is hope," the older man said.

"Hope?" Another man, younger, in his twenties, interjected. "The Americans are the reason we're in this mess! They funded the war against us and didn't do anything to stop the French from imposing those reparations! They only cared about getting their money back which is exactly what happened! And now look! What did they do? They gave us Hitler! The Americans are just as bad as the Nazis. What's the difference between any of them? Hitler? Stalin? Roosevelt? Chamberlain? They're all the same."

"You can't possibly be accusing the Americans for

what happened in Germany after the war, are you?" Matthias asked.

"Their President designed the terms of surrender and when France and England insisted on reparations, what did they do with the money paid to them by Germany? By the German people? They gave it to the United States! And when Hitler started to rise, what did they do? They figured out how much money they could get from him! The only thing Americans care about is money. Our safety? Not if they can profit off of our suffering. And that is exactly what they did in the 20's! Their banks made all these loans to Germany! Then their precious stock market crashes and what do the banks do? They recall the loans! Suddenly, Germany has no more money and what did Hitler do? He exploited that situation to his benefit! As long as there is greed in this world, we aren't safe anywhere."

The older man took a deep breath.

"Maybe so," the older man said as he finished his coffee. He reached into his pocket to get his money.

"It's on me," said Matthias. "It's alright."

The older man smiled and gave Matthias an appreciative nod as he straightened his jacket. He turned to the younger man and said something in Yiddish before leaving the cafe.

"What did he say?" Matthias asked.

"He said, 'I hope you're wrong.'"

Matthias lowered his head and proceeded to clean some coffee cups.

"I hope I'm wrong too," the young man said. Matthias looked up at him again. "I hope compassion for other men will once again come to humanity. I hope greed and hate will fall away and we will once again do what is right. Not motivated by personal gain but because it's the right thing to do. Too many people in this world think that by eliminating the sinner, they will in turn eliminate the sin. But there is always another sinner. If we can change our society so that no one will be tempted by sin, then we can all live as one. There is no greater sin than greed. Greed for wealth. Greed for power. Greed for fame. There's a mustached ape in Berlin who is suffering from those sins right now. We can't just get rid of him and think that everything will be alright. The virus that is affecting him is also affecting too many other people. Not only national leaders but also their followers and people who apologize for them. That is what we must eradicate, that sin, not the people. We need to change the way they see their fellow man to actually see them as their fellow man. That is what I hope and pray for because that is not the world we currently live in."

Matthias looked at the young man, his face expressionless but he felt a great deal of empathy. He genuinely did not know what to say to him.

"When you see a crooked tree," the young man began. "What do you think?"

"A crooked tree?"

"Say, you see a tree that has a bend in its trunk, what do you think when you see it?"

"I don't know, maybe it needed to reach sunlight."

"Exactly. Now, what do you think when you see a crooked person?" Matthias was silent. "When a tree is on the wrong path, it changes course to find the light and we do not think, 'what a disgusting tree!' When we see a person who is on the wrong path, we think, 'We must shun him!' Not enough people reach out to help someone see light and flourish."

Matthias and Camilla were sitting in their living room. As they sipped some Brandy, they listened to a Glenn Miller record playing on their phonograph. They sat in silence while they listened to the music of the American jazz musician. Matthias fell in love with jazz when he discovered the music while the Austrian National Team was playing in England. The melodies intoxicated him with excitement and a feeling of eternal youth. He found it impossible not to tap a toe to the beat. The tunes were simple and filled him with optimism. When he played the music for Camilla, she too, immediately fell in love with it.

"Your bruise is looking better," she said while gently brushing her finger over his cheek. The wound left from the punch he received from a Hitler supporter at mass had almost completely faded.

"It's nothing," he said with a smile. "I honestly almost forgot all about it."

Camilla smiled at him. She took another sip of brandy and took a deep breath.

"I wonder what some people in Berlin would think about us listening to American music," Camilla said in a joking manner.

"Don't say things like that," Matthias responded. Camilla put her Brandy down and stood in front of him and held out her hand.

"Dance with me, darling."

Matthias smiled, put his drink down, and stood to dance with his fiancee. As they let the music guide them, they swayed smoothly together. In love, in trance. Enjoying the moment they shared as a couple.

As Camilla motioned to hold him close to her by wrapping her arms around him in a loving embrace, he gently pulled away.

"Do you smell smoke?" he asked.

"What?" she was confused.

Matthias stopped dancing and looked around the house concerned. He turned off the music and walked around the house sniffing like a dog trying to find the source of the smell.

"Darling?" Camilla asked as she watched him walk from the kitchen to the hallway to the living room.

"There's a fire somewhere."

He then walked to the living room window. He peeked his head out of it and looked down the block. He could not see any flames but when he looked to the east, he stopped and focused. Even though the view was lit entirely by moonlight and streetlights, he was able to see a plume of smoke rising into the sky.

What he could not see was what was happening on the streets on which the fire was burning. Hordes of Nazi troops, Nazi supporters, and many others attacking the Jewish communities and neighborhoods of Vienna. Similar attacks were taking place across Germany and in recently conquered Nazi territories. In a speech the night before, Nazi Propaganda Minister Joseph Goebbels ordered that if riots were to happen in response to the vom Rath assassination that police should allow the rioters to have their way and not be impeded. Similar riots attacking Jewish communities were common in Central and Eastern Europe throughout the 18th and 19th Centuries. They were known as pogroms.

Matthias could not see from his apartment that they were looting and pillaging Jewish businesses and homes. He could not see that they were setting synagogues on fire. He could not see that they were beating, arresting, raping, and killing Jews who tried to fight back or who were just there, helpless victims. He did not know that the horrific events of that night would become known as Kristallnacht, the night of broken glass.

The next morning, Matthias saw the destruction that had occurred near his cafe. Glass from shattered windows littered the street. It was everywhere he looked. The smell of burning rock and cement filled the air. Smoke was still rising from the smoldering debris of synagogues and homes. Crying women clutched the bodies of husbands, brothers, and children who were shot or stabbed or beaten to death. Other people tried to clean up as much of the mess as they could. Their faces were blank, still in shock from what had happened mere hours earlier.

When fear, hopelessness, and anger become one emotion, it can paralyze one's spirit. The nervous system seems to break down and the person becomes merely an empty body. One man looked up at Matthias as he walked by. As they looked at each other, Matthias was struck at how expressionless the man's gaze was. It was as if his soul had been killed in the assault, leaving only the shell of a man.

As Matthias walked on, up and down the streets of his home city of Vienna, he was unable to recognize what he was looking at. Everything he saw was like a never-ending, all-consuming nightmare.

No coherent thoughts entered his head.

His mind was simply not working.

He deliberately placed one foot in front of the other, hearing the glass crack under the leather soles of his shoes.

The sounds of sorrow, cries of loss, and pain were the only things that he could comprehend.

"I wish they had just killed us all," someone behind Matthias said. He turned to look at who had spoken. He saw a woman, tears pouring from her eyes and down over her face. Her dress was stained with her husband's blood. He had been killed by a German machine gun as she watched helplessly. Her 10-year-old son tried to run away from the violence, but a Nazi car chased him down and ran him over. She had been up all night, holding both of their lifeless bodies, listening to the sound of gunshots, fire burning, and the wailing of wives becoming widows.

Matthias looked at her and froze. He did not know if he should try to comfort her or merely listen. He, himself, was in shock by the enormity of the scene in front of him.

"They blamed us for what happened in France!" she said hysterically. "I've never been to France! Almost everyone I know has never been out of the country. I could not even find France on a map. How can we be blamed for something that an idiot did?"

Matthias could no longer hold back his tears. He could not find any words to say. He wanted to hold the woman, console her in any way he could. As he motioned to hug her, she immediately rebuffed him.

"No!" she yelled. "I want to know why! I want to know why! What good does this do? What good does any of this do? What good is any of this? What does this prove? What have we done to deserve this?"

Another man approached her and tried to calm her down. She started sobbing hysterically while crying out, "why? why?" over and over again into his chest. Matthias looked on helplessly.

Standing amid the carnage, the despair, the confusion, the death, he realized the magnitude of the powers controlling his country. He felt that there was nothing more he could do to stop them. He scored a goal a few months before, but there were no goals for him to score now.

Matthias could still see, hear, and taste everything from the aftermath of Kristallnacht. It was the only thing that his mind centered on, he was oblivious to the rest of the world around him.

He didn't even realize it when he got to his cafe. The structure was still standing, but the front window was smashed out. The door was hanging by one screw in the hinge. He stepped inside carefully. It was clear someone had smashed up the bar, the walls, the tables with a sledgehammer. Wood shards were strewn everywhere. The vandals were not just trying to smash objects, they were trying to destroy the heart and soul of whatever they could.

As he walked through his cafe, he wrapped his arms around himself. A lump grew in his throat. He wanted to cry again. Not just shed tears of loss but he wanted to let out the wail of anguish that was burning a hole in his soul. He wanted to collapse and release everything he was feeling. The tears he cried for the woman were tears of empathy. This was a cry of anguish, of torment, of lost innocence.

With each breath he took, holding down the pain grew harder. He headed towards the back closet of the cafe to get his broom. With each step he took, a little peep, a tiny cry grew louder, piercing the silence. As a tear wet his cheek he came to the middle of his cafe. He stopped. He saw movement out of the corner of his eye. He looked and saw a little white mouse scurrying along the floorboards. Matthias dropped to his knees and watched it, wanting to scoop it up, to feel its little heartbeat warm his hands amidst all this devastation. Maybe, he thought, by holding this precious creature, he could be reminded of the joys of living again. This mouse, innocent and alive, had no idea what had happened the night before. Matthias smiled at the little creature, watching it forage for any scraps of food it could find.

"You aren't a Jew." Matthias snapped out of his state. He spun around and saw a young boy standing in the doorway. He looked at the youngster, his tunic unbuttoned, exposing a white undershirt. Short, curly locks of payot hung on either side of his head. Matthias immediately recognized the boy's garb as ethnically Jewish. "You aren't a Jew, are you?"

"No, I'm not." They stared at each other.

"Then we are all doomed to Hell."

The boy walked away.

"He's right," Matthias thought to himself. "If the Nazis attacked a business owned by a Christian, simply because it served Jews along with everyone else, then we are all doomed to Hell."

He thought back to when he bought the cafe. He felt that he was doing the right thing by buying this cafe so he could help Leopold, the Jewish man who owned the shop before him. He knew the German government hated Jews, that they wanted to make life difficult for Jews, and be rid of the Jews. They certainly did that to Leopold. But surely they would not interfere to this degree with Matthias' private business! Especially one as harmless as a small coffee shop. But he was wrong. They would smash windows and destroy the business simply to prove a point. But what point were they trying to prove? That they were stronger? Stronger than what? People who just want to live a peaceful life?

They did lose a stupid soccer game, after all, and then their goons started showing up at Matthias' shop. He could not help but wonder if all of this was because he would not conform. Was everyone being punished because of his defiance during an episode of sports entertainment?

Matthias looked back for the mouse but it had already vanished. Running away into the safety of its home, wherever that might be. Matthias was envious because even though he knew where his own home was, he no longer felt safe there. He no longer felt the comfort he once knew of being home, sure of what tomorrow would bring, certain of the brightness of a new day. He missed that feeling.

PART VII

"King of awful majesty,

Who freely savest the redeemed,

Save me, O fount of goodness."

—Wolfgang Amadeus Mozart, *Requiem*

I'm frightened," Matthias said to Camilla. They were walking together through the Burggarten, a beautiful and luscious garden and park in the middle of Vienna. It served as a refuge from the hustle and realities of city life for many people. It was built specifically to be that kind of sanctuary, taking its inspiration from Victorian England. It was a place where students could come to study, where the elderly could come to feed the ducks, or where couples could walk together in peace. But in recent days, peace was not something that could be found easily. The sense of hesitation and seriousness Camilla heard in Matthias' voice was a tone that she rarely ever heard from him.

The Jews, not only in Vienna but across the entirety of Germany's ever-expanding borders, were trying to clean up after Kristallnacht. They were also facing further humiliation and discrimination. Men and women, who the Nazis determined were fit enough, were arrested and sent to concentration camps to perform slave labor. Others were arrested and shot for almost any reason. Sometimes they were killed for a transgression as small as simply not answering a question fast enough, or giving a Nazi a look deemed inappropriate. It was not uncommon for the Viennese to see groups of Jewish people being forced by the Nazis to clean the streets on their hands and knees while the onlookers laughed and mocked them.

As they began their walk to the Burggarten, earlier in the day, Matthias and his fiancee passed such a scene. At least fifteen Jews, possibly a family, were lined up, shoulder to shoulder, on their hands and knees, visibly humiliated, scrubbing the road under the threatening gaze of a Gestapo officer who was rhythmically slapping a coiled whip in his palm. Other younger Gestapo, armed with powerful guns, were laughing at the scene before them.

"You missed a spot," an onlooker shouted in between his raucous laughter.

Camilla held Matthias' hand. She looked at the scene and then at him. His face was filled with horror but he was too afraid to say anything because of the frightening ugly relentlessness of the massive crowd. Matthias insisted that they leave and continue to walk over to the park. He felt utterly helpless. He knew that if he stepped in and tried to help those people that the Gestapo would target him either immediately or at some point. He already felt like a target was on his back.

"Another war is coming," Matthias said as they watched ducks land in the reflecting pond in the garden, creating ripples that continually reached the shore.

"England and France would never allow it," Camilla responded, trying to reassure him. "They're doing everything they can to avoid a war with Hitler."

"They're just emboldening him. The war is coming. It's only a matter of time."

Camilla pursed her lips and held his arm close to her in a loving embrace. She could tell that her efforts to reassure him were obviously failing. As they walked, Matthias began to slow down. He looked down a trail and was struck by what he saw in front of them. It was a memorial to Wolfgang Amadeus Mozart.

The musical genius wrote some of the most beloved, majestic, and famous orchestral and chamber pieces in the history of the Western world. From operas to symphonies and more. He died young. It is said that when he passed away, he was working on his final masterpiece, "Requiem."

There were whispers in certain circles that his death was no accident. Those whispers continued to persist that he did not die from consumption, or from some strange undiagnosed illness, but instead, that he was murdered by a jealous rival, the composer Antonio Salieri.

The memorial statue to Mozart stands at the center of the park. It shows a collection of cherubs at his feet, while the likeness of the young musical phenom holds a book of music in one hand, with the other hand open. It is as if he is offering his genius to the world to enjoy for all eternity. Matthias let go of Camilla's grip as he approached the composer's statue.

"They called me the 'Mozart of Football,'" he said without taking his eyes off the face of the statue. "It's funny though."

"What's funny, darling?"

"He and I really are very much alike."

"What do you mean?"

"Look at him. His stature. His frame is small. Beethoven was almost monstrous in comparison. But Mozart looks almost puny. He's a small man. Almost like me."

"Darling?"

"And he died a month before his thirty-sixth birthday. I'll be thirty-six in two months." He turned around and looked at his fiancee. "Think I'll make it past 36?"

"I know you will," she said while holding out her hand. "Now come on, I'm getting hungry. Let's go get something to eat and warm up."

Papers had started to pile up on the desk of Kriminalobersekretar Jurgen Schrempf. On top of one of the piles was a folder. It contained orders from his superiors. The Reich had decided to deal with what it called the Jewish Question, how to remove the entire Jewish population from their homes and communities, and relocating them to concentration camps. These camps were officially dubbed them "work camps," but they were really designed to effectively kill them off as quickly as possible. Along with the Jews, all the people Hitler decided were unnecessary for society, were included in these sinister plans, referring to them as parasites. People like homosexuals, Gypsies, the handicapped, and political enemies, were sent to these camps to be worked as slaves until they died. A few years later, the work fell by the wayside and mass extermination commenced with mechanical precision.

Schrempf opened the folder and read these new orders. He and his stormtroopers had to start arresting all identified Jews, any Jews who converted to Christianity, any Christians who were married to Jews, or anyone with a Jewish ancestor. He was to take them to the train station to be processed. Once there, they would be forcibly relocated to a camp in the east.

As the officer read this, he wondered about any of

the other undesirables in Austria. What of their apologists? He believed in Hitler's message. He believed that the Germans were the descendants of the Aryans and therefore part of a master race which must cleanse the Earth of all who were not of true Aryan blood. Anyone who did not agree was not just a political enemy, but a traitor to the cause of the Reich. It was a crime with only one punishment, death.

He stood up from his desk and walked over to the office of his superior, Kriminalkommissar Max Uhrmann.

"Heil Hitler!" he said with his arm raised. Uhrmann looked up from his desk, annoyed by the interruption.

"Heil Hitler," Uhrmann said with little enthusiasm. "What is it Schrempf?"

"These new orders for the preparation of the deportation of the Jews..."

"What of it?"

"What of the others?"

"Do your orders say anything of the others?"

"No, sir. I was wondering..."

"You're in no position to go above and beyond the call of duty, Schrempf."

"I understand." As Schrempf turned to leave, he held the door and then turned back to have one final word. "Sindelar's cafe was destroyed in the raids."

"Pity. I look forward to never hearing that man's name again."

Uhrmann looked back at his papers. When Schrempf did not immediately leave the office, he looked back up at his subordinate.

"Is there anything else, Schrempf?"

"No, Kriminalkommissar. Heil Hitler."

The young officer closed the door behind him and went back to his desk.

Schrempf sat down and looked out the window.

"What happened?" asked one of his colleagues, Otto Wurz.

"He doesn't care about Sindelar. But I fear that Sindelar is going to be trouble for us.

Wurz sat back in his chair and looked at Schrempf

"Jurgi," Wurz said delicately. "Don't you think we have more important matters at hand than dealing with a retired athlete who runs a cafe?"

"Perhaps. But we can't be too careful."

PART VIII

"He's the envy of the neighborhood: the professional athlete who escaped the factory of the office and gets paid to have fun."

—Eduardo Galeano, *Soccer in Sun and Shadow*

Snow began to cover the ground as children laughed and played. They threw snowballs, made snow angels, and created snowmen. The infectious glee of children enjoying the snowfall is the familiar sign that Christmas would arrive soon.

The weeks before Christmas is a special time of year. Even though the air is cold, there is a warmth emanating from everyone. It is as if they are taking the freezing air and turning it, almost magically into something positive. They do not let the gloom of the weather bring them down. They welcome the snow as a symbol of the holiday season.

Matthias was able to clean up his cafe and get the front pane of glass replaced. He placed a wreath on the door, a gesture in honor of the holidays. The clientele he was now serving were not from the nearby neighborhood. He could tell, based on how they were dressed, that they were upper-class Viennese who wanted to share the same room as the famous sports hero. They were not interested in talking about the news of the day. Instead, they wanted to hear about his days filled with sporting glory.

"What actually happened against Italy?" someone

asked, referring to the fateful match in the semi-finals against the host nation in the 1934 World Cup. It is believed by many that Italian dictator Benito Mussolini bribed the referees to make sure Austria lost, preventing the team from reaching the finals.

"We were robbed," he responded.

"Did you ever play in Moscow?" another patron asked.

"No, I haven't."

Word soon got around the various social circles of Vienna that the great Matthias Sindelar was as accessible as anyone. Matthias capitalized upon this and rechristened the Cafe Annahof as Cafe Sindelar making it a hotspot for many people.

On one cold December morning, a noticeably handsome man walked into the cafe. He was wearing a tailored tweed suit and was sporting a thin mustache. When he saw Matthias standing behind the bar washing coffee cups, he approached him with a stroll that oozed confidence and bravado. He sat at the bar and stared openly at the former football star."What can I get for you?"

"Cappuccino, please."

As Matthias prepared the beverage, he could feel the man's eyes on him.

"How are you liking this weather?" he asked to ease the tension which now inevitably preceded any conversation with a stranger.

"It's refreshing. Tell me something."

"Yes?"

"Have you ever done what you do on camera?" Matthias turned around and gave the man a confused look.

"I beg your pardon?"

"I'm sorry, I don't think I introduced myself. I'm Johann von Vasary," he held out his hand. Matthias reached his out as well and they began to shake hands. "And you are the great Matthias Sindelar!"

"I am." Matthias tried to look humble. He was struck by the confidence in the strength of the man's handshake.

"I'm making a movie here in Vienna and I have a role that would be perfect for you."

"Are you serious?" Matthias was flattered and a little embarrassed. "Would I be playing a cafe owner?"

"No, no, no," Johann was laughing a little. "You'd be playing you. The part is of Matthias Sindelar and I want you to portray yourself on the big screen! Envision it! The great Matthias Sindelar immortalized on the big screen for all the world to see!"

The director knew that by appealing directly to the ego, this was a surefire way to turn any amount of reluctance into a yes.

"What's the movie called?" Matthias asked.

"It's called 'Roxy und das Wunderteam!'" With both hands, he motioned as if he were concocting the movie's sign out of thin air. "Rosi Barsony is starring!"

Rosi Barsony was quite the star in the 20's and throughout the 30's in Europe. She had starred in more than a dozen films at that point and her beauty made the silver screen shine. The film was a musical and the plot was extremely simple. It was about a woman who falls in love with a soccer player. The movie was really more about the music than it was about football. In fact, the songs featured had nothing to do with the plot. If the songs were not there, the film would have been about thirty minutes long. But it was pure, silver screen entertainment at its finest. Vasary wanted Matthias to think he was going to be in Germany's version of "Gone With The Wind," when in fact he was going to be in a simple B-movie.

Matthias was intrigued. But before he could ask another question, Johann handed him an envelope.

"It will be one day of shooting, and you'll be handsomely compensated, of course."

Matthias opened the envelope and unfolded the offer letter which sat inside. It was an official contract. All the terms had been printed up and it was just awaiting Matthias' signature. Obviously, Johann had anticipated Matthias' wholehearted agreement to the deal even before he broached it. And he had been right. Matthias did not read the entire agreement, only noticing the bold black ink that showed what he would be paid. It was an offer for more money than what he earned with Wien in his entire last year of professional play. It would be more than enough to pay for his wedding to Camilla and their honeymoon, something they could already afford, but now there was no need to be frugal with how extravagant Camilla wanted it to be.

"You'd only need me for a day?"

"Just one day."

Johann, in dramatic fashion, extracted a fountain pen from his jacket pocket. He slid it across the bar to Matthias. He took the pen and signed his name on the signature section of the contract.

"Excellent!" Johann said enthusiastically. "The address of the studio is on the contract. See you tomorrow?"

"See you tomorrow."

M atthias showed up on set the next morning and did not know what to expect. He had never been on a movie set before. He looked around for Johann but did not know where to find him. He approached a young page and asked where the director was. He was directed to the door leading outside.

Matthias walked through the exit doors and was taken aback by what he saw in front of him. A giant painting, at least twenty feet high, of a packed stadium with cheering fans. In the foreground, leading up to it was a grass soccer pitch.

He saw actors and extras walking around in soccer uniforms. Those who were not in costume were wearing denim overalls carrying lights or camera equipment. One was carrying a ladder.

"It's going to look great on screen," Johann said as he wrapped his arm around Matthias' shoulder, startling him. "Listen, I'm going to need you to get into makeup and costume, we want to be able to wrap by 3. Rosi is, well, she's Rosi. She's refusing to be emotionally available right now."

"I don't understand."

"It's ok. Greta! Greta!" Johann was calling for the costume designer. "Can you please show Matthias to his dressing room?"

As Matthias was escorted through the set to his dressing room, he noticed that some actors were wearing uniforms colored red and white and others in vertical black and white stripes, reminiscent of the Italian club Juventus.

"Am I playing against Juventus in this movie?" he asked with a smirk on his face.

"Actually, darling, I have no idea," Greta said as

she pulled out Matthias's uniform for the shoot. A red and white shirt and white shorts. "I just designed the costumes. This should fit you."

Matthias took the clothes and stepped into his dressing room. He closed the door behind him and looked in the mirror. He unbuttoned his shirt and hung it up on the hook. He then took off his pants and pulled on the shorts. Then he took the shirt he would be wearing for the shoot and put it on.

When he saw himself in the mirror wearing that shirt, his shoulders instinctively broadened. He had not worn a soccer uniform in over a year and his body still responded the same way. He was proud to be a soccer player. In his soul, he missed that feeling of wearing the uniform. He missed being able to express himself playing the game he loved.

He looked closely at the crest on the shirt and smiled when he did not see a swastika anywhere on it.

He stepped out of the dressing room and heard clapping. He looked over and saw it was coming from Johann.

"There's my star!"

Matthias smiled and brushed his hand over his shirt to straighten it a little. He was trying to show that the unfamiliar surroundings were not intimidating him.

"Matthias, this is your opponent for today's game.

Hans Holt, Matthias Sindelar."

Hans, dressed in the black and white uniform, reached out his hand to shake Matthias'. He was an up and coming actor in central Europe. With his strong, square jaw and traditional Hollywood good looks, Hans quickly made Matthias feel at ease.

"I'm a huge fan of yours, Der Papierene," Hans said. There was a hint of bashfulness in his voice. Obviously, this movie star was nervous around his sports idol.

"I'm a huge fan of yours as well," Matthias said. In truth, he had not yet heard of Hans. Even though Matthias was a well-known celebrity and friends with many celebrities, he did not know everyone.

"Now here's how the scene is going to play out," Johann said. He told Matthias that he wanted to get a few shots of him getting the ball past Hans before shooting a goal. Then he wanted to get some close-ups of Matthias watching the ball go into the net.

"Think you got it?" Johann asked.

"I think so," Matthias responded. He was more confused than he was before.

He stepped onto the fake pitch and was handed a soccer ball. He instinctively placed it on the ground and started passing it back and forth between his feet.

"Not yet, Matthias, we haven't started rolling yet,"

Johann said.

"Sorry."

Hans stepped in front of Matthias and got into a defensive position, with his legs open wide and his arms outstretched.

"Now Matthias, you're going to get the ball around Hans and run past him. Ready? And, action!"

Matthias instinctively dribbled the ball between his left and right foot, trying to trick his opponent into going in the opposite direction. It was like he was back in his childhood neighborhood playing with his friends. He kicked the ball through Hans' legs and ran around him. Then caught the ball with his feet.

"That was great! Now shoot!"

Matthias kicked the ball and saw it fly into the top corner of the goalmouth. The net caught the ball and Matthias gave himself a huge smile. Another actor playing the coach stood on the side of the pitch and clapped his hands together.

"Matthias, run over and shake his hand!"

He ran over and the pair shook hands. They patted each other on the back. Hans shook his head and frowned.

"Good Hans! Do that again!"

Hans repeated the action.

"Cut! Did we get all that?" Johann asked the cinematographer. He gave the director a thumbs-up.

"Terrific! Matthias, we're going to do that again. But this time, with more feeling."

Matthias did the same exact play over and over again, at least fifteen times. By the end of the day, he was exhausted both physically and mentally.

Johann thanked him for appearing in his film and handed him a check.

"Do you want to keep the costume?" Johann asked him.

"Sure, why not?" Matthias thought it would be fun to frame it and hang it in his cafe. He hoped that one day people will ask him about the day he met the famous movie star Hans Holt, instead of the incessant questions about playing against Italy in the 1934 World Cup.

As he stepped off the set, he saw an unwelcome figure waiting for him. The Gestapo officer Kriminalobersekretär Jurgen Schrempf.

"Herr Sindelar?"

"Yes?"

"I'm very curious about you."

"Do I know you?"

"Kriminalobersekretär Jurgen Schrempf. I'm with the Gestapo. I've been keeping an eye on you."

"Well, thank you for protecting me. But I can take care of myself."

"Yes, you're a big movie star now."

"I'm sorry, Herr Schrempf. But am I under arrest?"

"Not yet. But you may be of some service to our endeavors."

"I don't think so. I just want to mind my own business." Matthias started walking to the car that was waiting for him.

"All you need to do is let us know what the Jews in your cafe are talking about."

"You want to know what the people in my cafe are talking about? They want to know what it was like when I was playing against Manchester United or the against Scottish National Team. Or what happened when Mussolini robbed us of the World Cup. They ask if they can have more cream for their coffee. Sometimes they ask about their neighbors and family members because one of them mysteriously vanished." Matthias opened the back door of the car and turned around for one final word, "That's assuming there are any Jews left in Vienna."

"We're not done yet, Sindelar."

"What else would you like to know?"

"I understand that you're a Czech national."

Matthias looked at the officer curiously who was now uncomfortably close to him.

"I was born in Kozlov which is now in Czechoslovakia but I am an Austrian." He paused for a moment before continuing with his answer. "An Austrian who is now German."

"Are you a Socialist? Communist? Capitalist?"

"I don't get involved in politics. I'm a retired footballer who now owns a cafe. Are we done now?"

"For now."

Matthias got in the back of the car and told the driver to go.

"Rapid was always better than Wien anyways," Schrempf said to himself and walked to his car.

In the car, Matthias was shaking. His nerves were rattled from the chance meeting he had with the Gestapo. He wiped away beads of sweat from his brow with his handkerchief. His knees still shook and his right leg bounced up and down because of the stress of the meeting. He just wanted to go home.

"Do you need to stop anywhere before I drop you off Herr Sindelar?" the driver asked him.

"Is there a grocer nearby?"

"Around the corner."

"Do they sell liquor?"

He picked up a package of sausages, a bottle of champagne, and a small bottle of schnapps, which he drank on the way home. The booze cooled his nerves, allowing him to take a deep breath. Once he got home and walked through the door, he finally felt like he could relax.

"There's my movie star," Camilla said with a big smile and a bigger hug.

"I'm starving," Matthias responded. He placed the paper bag on the counter and pulled out the sausages.

"Darling, the oven is completely kaput."

"Then let's replace it." Matthias crossed his arms and leaned against the counter. He looked at the old oven and shook his head. "We can afford it now."

"Oh stop, you big Hollywood dreamer! We'll just get the Allrounder to fix it. Why waste money?"

"I've asked him to fix it a hundred times!" Matthias threw his head back in frustration. "All he ever tells me is that he'll get around to it. That man is lazier than a pig in the summertime."

"Ask him again. If he doesn't do it this time, then we'll buy a new one."

Matthias reluctantly agreed and they went out to a restaurant for dinner. That night, she could sense a change in the mood of the man she loved. For the last few weeks, she sensed a dark cloud hanging over him. His mood was now less melancholy. She started to recognize him again. Maybe it was as simple as being on the movie set, being surrounded by people boosting his ego by telling him how great he was, something that he had not experienced since his playing days. Whatever the reason was, she did not want this mood to vanish. She did not want to see his face sour again.

The next morning, before Matthias left for the cafe, he banged on the door of his building's Allrounder.

"Andreas," Matthias yelled as he banged. "Andreas, it's Sindelar!"

The door opened slightly and the portly middle-aged man peeked his head through the opening. He leaned his body against the door frame, taking the weight from his belly off of his hips and knees. He pushed his glasses up but they immediately slipped down his nose again.

"You're asking about your stove again?" he asked.

"I am. Will you be able to get it fixed?"

"Because it's Christmas, I doubt that I'll be able to get all the right tools I need. I might need to wait until after the New Year."

"Andreas, I've been asking you for weeks to get this fixed."

"I know. But I have a whole building to take care of. I can't fix everything at the snap of a finger."

"Look, please at least figure out what tools you'll need soon. We're tired of not having a stove to cook on."

"I'll see what I can do."

The door closed and Matthias walked out of the apartment building shaking his head. Once outside, he put his leather gloves on and his fedora on as he made his way to the cafe.

Watching him walk away was Jurgen Schrempf, who was parked across the street in a black Mercedes. The Gestapo got out of the car. He was wearing the familiar gray overcoat tightened with a waist belt. He put his hat on and walked into Matthias' building. He walked right up to the door of the Allrounder.

"I said I'd see what I can do!" Andreas' shouted through the door before opening it. He was taken aback by the sight of a Gestapo officer in full uniform standing before him.

"Herr Fennegar, I assume?"

"Ya," the Allrounder said nervously. "I am Herr Fennegar."

"Matthias Sindelar is a tenant here correct?"

"Ya. I was just speaking with him about his stove."

"I am Kriminalobersekretär Jurgen Schrempf. I am investigating Herr Sindelar."

Visibly frightened, the Allrounder began to stammer with his words as he tried to make sense of the situation.

"I do not rent any of my apartments to Jews, never have!" he said with as much confidence as he could muster. "If Sindelar is a Jew, I was completely unaware. I saw him go to church even!"

"I know, Herr Fennenger," Schrempf said with a

disarming smile. "You are a good patriot to the Reich. May I please come in?"

Andreas opened the door a little wider and stepped aside, allowing the officer room to step past him.

"Your apartment is quite comfortable, Herr Fennenger." Schrempf walked in with his hands behind his back, looking around the Allrounder's home. Andreas quickly picked up some newspapers which were laying around in a hasty, yet futile attempt to straighten up for his unexpected guest. "It could use a woman's touch, obviously."

"My wife passed away some years ago."

"My condolences."

Schrempf sat down on the couch and carefully and meticulously removed his leather gloves. He pulled at each of the fingertips before removing the glove entirely.

"Herr Fennenger," Schrempf began. "Sindelar is not under suspicion of being a Jew. I've personally researched his lineage and any Jewish blood that he could possibly possess has thankfully been diluted. In the eyes of the Reich, Sindelar is not a Jew. However, there are some questions with regard to his—shall we say—loyalty to his nation."

Schrempf looked Andreas in the eye. He could see that his host was concerned by what he was hearing.

"I assume you are aware of his actions at the

Celebration of Unity Match, the Anschluss Match," Schrempf asked.

"I am."

"He also recently purchased a cafe from a Jew in Favoriten?"

"I've heard about it. I've not been there yet."

Schrempf sat back in his seat.

"Some of his clientele have been questionable. In delicate situations like this, the Reich could use the help of someone who can obtain intimate knowledge of any dissident aggressors."

"I would like to help," Andreas said enthusiastically. "If there is a traitor to the nation in my building, I will do anything possible to protect my most patriotic tenants and the good people of this nation!"

"When was the last time you spoke to him?"

"Earlier. Just a few minutes ago."

"What did you two speak about?"

"His stove. He needs it repaired."

"When do you plan on repairing his stove?"

"Soon. I just need to make sure that I have all the tools I need."

"When you visit their home, please feel free to look around. Report to me about what you see. What are the books or magazines that they collect? What is written in their diaries and journals? These are the things that we need to know. We cannot take anything for granted."

"I will do what I can."

"I know you will, Herr Fennenger. The Reich is lucky to have a citizen like you. I wish more people were as enthusiastic about supporting and helping ensure the safety of our society. Without the help that you're providing, the mission of our Fuhrer could very well be in jeopardy."

Schrempf pulled out his business card from his pocket and handed it to Andreas before standing up. He walked towards the door to let himself out.

"I look forward to hearing from you."

Andreas kept an eye on his window. He was waiting for Camilla to leave. Once he saw her walk out of the building later in the morning, he collected his toolbox and marched up the stairs to their apartment. In front of the door, he pulled out his handkerchief and wiped some sweat from his brow. He was winded from the hike up the stairs, but he was also having trouble controlling his racing heart. He was excited to be on a mission to help his government. He fantasized about the possibility of receiving a reward for his efforts, even though none was promised to him.

He then pulled out his master key and let himself

in. He placed the toolbox on the counter and started to walk around the home. He was looking for anything that the Gestapo could find suspicious.

He looked at the bookshelf first, there were a few popular novels, a few cookbooks, and a few books about history.

"Hmm," he thought to himself. "This one is about American history!"

He wrote the titles down in a small notebook.

On the bottom shelf, he found their record collection. Jazz records. More specifically, jazz by American black musicians. He made sure to record this find in his notebook. He even underlined it and put a star next to it.

He walked into the bedroom and found what looked like a journal on the nightstand. He assumed that it belonged to Camilla because of the printed floral pattern on the cover. He sat down on the bed, picked up the diary, and opened it to a random page.

"Is this in Italian?" he exclaimed out loud. He closed the book and placed it back on the nightstand. He wrote in his notebook that he found a journal but could not understand what was written. He did not find a journal on the other side of the bed.

He then walked back into the kitchen and pulled the stove out of its place. He looked at the connection and fiddled with some of the knobs. He then tore a piece of paper out of his notebook.

He wrote down, "Looked at your stove. I think I know what's wrong. Will need different tools. Will return."

He left the apartment without putting the stove back.

Jurgen Schrempf sat at his desk going over evidence papers when his phone rang. It was Andreas calling to report what he had just found.

"That's good, Andreas," he said into the phone. "How many would you say?"

He wrote down what he heard, taking copious notes.

"I, on behalf of a grateful nation, thank you for your efforts," he hung up the phone and looked over at Otto. "I think we finally have something on Sindelar!"

He stood up excitedly and ran towards Uhrmann's office.

"What?" Otto got up and followed his partner.

"Herr Kriminalkommissar," Jurgen said to his superior.

"What is it, Schrempf?" Uhrmann looked up from his typewriter and sat back in his chair.

"I have something important that you need to see."

Schrempf walked into the office and placed his notes on his superior's desk. Otto stood in the doorway looking confused.

Uhrmann looked at the notes regarding the items the Allrounder found in Sindelar's apartment. He then looked past Schrempf and directly at Otto.

"What do you make of Sindelar?" Uhrmann asked.

"Obviously, he's a well-loved celebrity. I know he just made a movie. He has taken some questionable stances towards the Reich. But lately, quite honestly, it seems like he's mostly keeping to himself."

"These questionable stances," Uhrmann stood and walked over to Schrempf. "Do you think they amount to treason?"

Jurgen's head spun around. His eyes were wide. In his mind, he was screaming, "YES! He's a traitor!" He was trying to will that answer into the mouth of his partner.

"Treason?" Otto began. "I believe that Matthias Sindelar is being used as a symbol for those who are traitors and who might one day commit treason. But has he done anything treasonous? I have not seen any evidence that would stand up in court, Herr Kriminalkommissar."

"Neither have I," Uhrmann pressed Schrempf's notebook into the officer's chest. Jurgen's hands came up to grab it, keeping it from falling to the floor. "American history books and Negro music? Sindelar might have questionable musical taste. He might be a tad bit defiant against our efforts. But give me something more than this if you want me to sign off on bringing him in for treason. For crying out loud, Schrempf, I own books about American history!"

Uhrmann sat back down behind his desk.

"But," Jurgen tried to find the words to respond. "As Otto said, he's becoming a symbol of the resistance! His cafe is becoming more popular!"

Uhrmann took a deep breath and was becoming increasingly annoyed.

"Why do you really think there's something there?" he asked.

"He's a Czech national…"

"He's Czech?" Uhrmann interrupted.

"He was born in Kozlov."

"Kozlov was part of Austria before the War!"

"I know, but also…"

"But also what? You're wasting my time."

"He's extremely sympathetic to Jews, communists, and socialists."

"Sympathetic? What does 'sympathetic' mean?"

"We know that there are some people throughout the nation who are hiding Jews and trying to protect them from relocation. There are people who are helping them. We know this. We're intercepting money coming in from

American Jew supporters who are trying to send these funds to criminal elements here in the Fatherland. We know based on Sindelar's behavior at the Anschluss match that he is not loyal to the Furhrer. We know that before the cleansing of our cities that Sindelar served Jews in his cafe. We know that he continues to do so. And if Sindelar is somehow aiding in this treason, he can help us catch other Jewish sympathizers who are protecting the criminals. As far as I am concerned, he is an enemy who needs to be shown the error of his ways and forced to become an ally."

"You think Sindelar has information about this conspiracy?"

"He might." Schrempf, in truth, had no evidence connecting Sindelar to the efforts of the Americans or the British or anyone else trying to get Jews out of Germany. Several Jewish communities, and anti-fascist communities, were sending money, forged passports, forged work visas, anything, to get friends and loved ones who were trapped by the Nazis out of Europe and to freedom. Sometimes, those correspondences were intercepted by the Gestapo which meant certain death for the people they were meant to help.

"Alright," Max said finally and reluctantly. "Put a surveillance team at the cafe. But don't come back into this office until you have something more solid than a bunch of jazz records and history books."

PART IX

"When the Christmas bells sounded in the villages of the Vosges behind the lines... something fantastically unmilitary occurred. German and French troops spontaneously made peace and ceased hostilities; they visited each other through disused trench tunnels, and exchanged wine, cognac and cigarettes for Westphalian black bread, biscuits and ham."

—Richard Schirrmann, December 1915

The days immediately before and after Christmas and New Year's Day are supposed to be a joyous time. Smiles are usually on everyone's faces. The merriment is supposed to be infectious.

As 1938 drew to a close, no one could have or wanted to predict that another major war was months away. The scars of the last war were still fresh, and its long, deep wound still lingered. In some parts of Europe, the war never really ended, as civil wars, revolutions and border disputes raged.

Yet, a mere twenty-three years earlier, the Great War was briefly suspended. After the First Battle of Ypres, one of the War's bloodiest battles, leaders of the opposing armies crossed no-man's land to discuss a cease-fire over the Christmas holiday. During the cease-fire, the soldiers laid down their arms and played football against each other. A peaceful battle where differences were settled not in a body count but instead in goals scored.

When Jules Rimet, the President of FIFA, created the World Cup, he said that the tournament could help prevent wars from being fought because the sport of football helps bring nations together. Even though the sport helped bring about a brief cessation of hostilities during the Great War, the battles continued to rage on and it practically tore Europe apart.

When 1938 became 1939, when the clock struck midnight, Camilla swung her arms around Matthias' neck and kissed him deeply. They were at a party with other celebrities and hangers-on drinking too much champagne and expensive wine. The buzz from the holiday excitement and the alcohol numbed their nerves and allowed them to forget about the government officials stalking them. The sight of the black Mercedes was becoming so common, they simply stopped noticing after a while.

Matthias broke away from her kiss and looked around the room for a moment.

"Are you suddenly growing modest on me?" Camilla asked.

"I thought someone was watching."

She grabbed his chin and forced him to look at her.

"Stop worrying," she ordered. "I want to enjoy this night without thinking about them."

Matthias smiled and held her tighter. They kissed again and then she rested her cheek against his.

"Take me home," she whispered in his ear.

He smiled and took her hand. They navigated their way out of the party and went home. Once there, he grabbed hold of her and carried her into their bed. She ran her fingers through his hair and down his neck to his shoulders. She then found his collar and began to unbutton it as he kissed her passionately. He lifted her dress as he gently began undressing her.

"I can't wait to be your wife," she whispered to him.

"I can't wait to make you my wife," he responded.

Their embrace filled the room with energy and love. The touch they shared, the bond they wished to make sacred, was already present. She felt the love he had for her and he felt the love she had for him. At this moment, this one precious moment in time, they were one.

As the sun began to rise, in her sleep, Camilla traced her finger around his knuckle. She felt warm in his arms. At this moment she was happy. Since the pair met, she thought, she was always happy because he was always in her thoughts.

But she was pulled out of this early morning dream by the sound of pounding on the door. The banging was furious and loud.

"Sindelar!" came the angry shout from the other side of the door. "Open the door immediately!"

"What is that?" Matthias said in a haze. He rubbed some of the sleep out of his eyes as he searched for his bathrobe. He could barely keep his balance because of his heavy hangover. He struggled to tie his robe as he approached the door.

The banging stopped as he unlocked the door. When he opened it, he recognized the man standing before him. It was Jurgen Schrempf. The Gestapo was accompanied by Otto and a dozen other officers.

"We need to search your apartment," Schrempf said as he pushed Matthias out of the way and let himself in, the other officers followed. Matthias looked at them confused. He looked back to the bedroom and saw Camilla fumbling with her robe as she got it on.

"What is this about?" he asked.

"We are looking for anti-Aryan contraband," Schrempf responded.

One of the officers pulled records off of his shelf. One by one, he pulled out the vinyl from the cardboard cover sleeve, tossing them on the floor. Schrempf walked over and picked up one of the records. He held it up to his face and read the label.

"Duke Ellington?" he said while he looked at Matthias. "Why would someone want to listen to the music of an American Negro?"

"I don't understand," Matthias said.

Schrempf, still holding the record, walked over to the dining table and smashed it over the edge, breaking it into a dozen pieces.

"It's unacceptable."

Other Gestapo pulled photos out of frames and tore up photo albums. They pulled books off the shelves, tossing them on the floor. All of their possessions were now littered across the apartment.

Otto walked up to Jurgen.

"Kriminalobersekretar," he said. "We have a diary, a few receipts, and a datebook. A few other questionable items that we will need to review further. Not much else."

Schrempf looked over at the stove, which was still pulled out of its place. He walked into the kitchen and opened the oven to look inside.

"That's not working properly," Matthias said nervously. He was trying to make sense of what was happening and fearing the worst might happen. "We're still waiting for the Allrounder to fix it."

Schrempf then looked at the back of the appliance. He looked inside the drilled holes where the gas lines go into the wall. He tapped on them and pulled on the cords. Matthias and Camilla looked on quizzically. Finally, after what seemed like an eternity to the couple, Schrempf stood up.

"Thank you for your time, Paper Man" he said

mockingly. "We'll need to review what we've found."

He stood in the doorway while the Gestapo left the apartment with some of their belongings. Schrempf closed the door behind him. Matthias and Camilla stared at the back of their front door in deep shock. They were completely confused about what had just happened. They did not understand what the Gestapo was looking for or why they confiscated Camilla's diary or their datebook.

"What on Earth just happened?" Matthias wondered. Camilla glared at him.

"Is there anything you want to tell me?" she asked pointedly. The tone in her voice made Matthias think she suspected something. The muscles in his shoulders tensed and he suddenly felt extremely defensive. "What are they looking for?"

"I have no idea."

"Are you doing anything at your cafe?"

"Darling, what are you talking about?"

"Don't darling me! Are you protecting Jews? Are you helping them escape?"

"Why are you..."

"Are you doing something that is going to get us killed?"

"No, for Heaven's sake, no!"

"Then why are they harassing us? Why would they do this?"

"God damn it, I don't know!" Matthias screamed in anger. It was a scream he could not hold back. Camilla looked at him and slowly, reluctantly, became disarmed. As her own anger and frustrations started to cool, she broke her gaze away from Matthias to look at the mess that was left behind.

"We should clean this up," she said.

She walked into the bedroom and found a clean pair of pajamas to throw on. Matthias picked up a photo of himself as a child holding his first soccer ball. It was brown and made of pure cow leather. He looked at his little fingers touching the stitching. He remembered when that picture was taken. His uncle had just purchased a Kodak camera, imported from America. It was quite expensive and he always bragged about how much it cost him. As Matthias looked at this boy holding the ball in the photo, he felt an ache deep inside of him. His foot missed the feel of kicking a ball. He missed the days of innocence and being able not to worry about what he thought, what he read, or who he served coffee to. He missed being able to dream only of sporting glory.

Now, all his dreams were nightmares. Nightmares, constant terror, merciless dread, were the only things circulating in his mind.

PART X

"But the idol is an idol only for a moment, a human eternity, all of nothing; and when the time comes for the golden foot to become a lame duck, the star will have completed his journey from sparkle to blackout."

—Eduardo Galeano, *Soccer in Sun and Shadow*

atthias and Camilla no longer felt comfortable in their own home. They started going on more walks, finding any excuse not to be at home. When Matthias was not at his cafe, they would spend time at other restaurants or cafes or theaters. The pair found any excuse possible not to be at home.

"Maybe we should go to Switzerland like Walter," Matthias offered once.

"Maybe," Camilla replied. "But let's discuss this later."

The days were becoming shorter as winter continued on. Matthias was smiling less. Whenever he did smile, it was out of obligation not out of joy. Coming home was a difficult thing for both of them to do now, but they always had to. There was always a heavy sigh and trepidation before they opened the door.

Then, one day, they came home to find the door slightly ajar. Matthias' heart skipped a beat. He felt a cold chill come over him. He looked at Camilla. Her eyes were wide and her lower lip was quivering. Matthias forced his eyes to focus as he slowly pushed the door open. As it creaked open, he held his breath. He breathed a sigh of relief when he saw Andreas sitting on the floor working on their stove.

"Andreas," Matthias said becoming calm. "I wasn't expecting you."

"I knocked," he responded. "But I knew that you were anxious to get this fixed and I had the tools now. So, I let myself in. I apologize for the inconvenience."

"It's quite alright," he said giving Camilla a reassuring glance. "Is the stove fixed now?"

"Yes, Herr Sindelar. I'm almost done."

The couple walked into their home and took off their jackets and hung them on the pegs. Andreas pulled out a small wrench and tightened a bolt in the back of the stove. Then, after returning the tool to his bag, he jumped to his feet and returned the stove to its spot.

"It should be working fine for you now," the Allrounder said.

"Thank you so much, Andreas," Camilla said. "What was wrong with it?

"One of the lines needed to be replaced." Andreas collected his tool bag, grabbed a large paper bag, and walked to the door. "Before I forget..."

He reached into the large paper bag and pulled out a bottle of Grants whiskey.

"I picked this up for you and the Fraulein as an

apology for the delay with the repairs."

"That is very kind of you," Matthias said. "Thank you very much, Andreas."

After they shook hands, Andreas left the apartment and Matthias closed the door. He and Camilla were alone.

"Do you think the stove is really fixed?"

"So he says," while he turned on one of the burners and they saw a flame ignite.

J urgen's desk was becoming buried in papers. He was trying to make sense of all the work he had ahead of him when his phone rang. The clanging bell increased his stress too. He threw his hands up in frustration as he tried to find his phone on his crowded desk. He picked up the receiver and held it to his ear.

"This is Schrempf."

"I have a breakdown of what the diary read," said the voice on the other end.

"Yes."

"It's a collection of her dreams. She was falling, she was swimming, she was running away from alligators. That's basically it."

"What are you talking about?" Schrempf was furious.

"I'm sorry, sir. But that was all there was. Nothing

about her relationship, nothing about her views on the government. Nothing of the sort."

Jurgen slammed the phone down in anger. He crossed his arms and stared out the window.

"Not what you wanted to hear," Otto asked.

"There is no way that Uhrmann would ever sign off on bringing Sindelar in now."

"Jurgi, face it. He's just got a bad attitude. Just accept that he's not working with our nation's enemies."

"We're going to find something on him. One way or another he is working against the Fatherland and he will pay for his petulance."

Matthias had just closed up his cafe for that day's business, but he was not closing up entirely for the night. He was hosting some close friends, old and new, for a get-together. Poker, cigars, gossip, and plenty of laughs.

"Der Papierine!" was what his friends would say as they walked into the cafe. His teammates from the Wunderteam like Karl Sesta and Josef Smistik showed up with their wives and greeted their friend with big hugs. Old friends from his days at Austria Wien, Egon Ulbrich, and Gustav Hartmann, two people he had not seen since he retired from football, did the same.

"Matthias," Egon began after shaking hands. "I have an important question to ask you."

"Yes," he responded. "What is it? Anything."

"Doctor Michl. Have you heard anything from him?"

"I have not. But last I heard, he and his wife made their way to France."

"Thank goodness. Thank goodness."

The men sat at a table and began their poker game. The wives sat at another table. Placed in the center of the men's table was a bottle of Schnapps. Matthias poured each of his friends a glass.

"Have you heard?" Matthias began. "Hitler is trying to get Germany to host the next World Cup."

"I doubt FIFA would go for it," Karl replied. "The last two were in Europe. They'll put it back in South America."

"I think the next one should be in Egypt," Joseph said with a laugh. "We can play a game in front of the pyramids!"

They all laughed, enjoying each other's company and stupid jokes, and Matthias dealt them all another game.

"Have you ever heard of Wild Bill Hickok?" Matthias asked while looking at his cards. He held two aces, two eights, and a three.

"The cowboy?" Karl asked confused.

"Yes, I read a book about him a few years ago."

Matthias placed one card, face down, on the table. The move implied that he was going to get just one new card for his hand. The other men sitting around the table followed suit and they all placed cards they wanted to trade in on the table and also placed chips in for their bets.

"What about him?" Joseph asked.

Matthias took a sip of his Schnapps and gently adjusted his cards between his thumb and fingers. He took his new card and adjusted it so it sat comfortably in his hand.

"He was playing poker in a Western saloon somewhere in 1876 one afternoon."

Matthias placed another chip in the center of the table upping his bet.

"I'm out," Karl said. Josef and Gustav also folded. Only Egon remained.

"Ok, so Wild Bill Hickok was playing poker one day in America," Egon said, staring his friend in the eye. "What about it?"

"While he was playing, he was shot in the back of the head by some drunk. What cards was he holding?"

"Tell me," Egon said.

"A pair of aces and a pair of eights," Matthias presented those exact cards to the table. "They call this

'The Dead Man's Hand.'"

He started chuckling and some of the other men joined in with his laughter.

"Two pair," Egon said. "That's a good hand."

"It is, isn't it."

"But it's not as good as a full house."

Egon presented his hand, three tens and a pair of fours. Everyone at the table clapped and burst out with laughter. "Pay up, Paper Man!"

The card game went on well into the night. Matthias looked around the table and felt like he was at home. These friends were his brothers. They were teammates, colleagues, neighbors. These were men he could count on when he needed someone. Having them in his life rejuvenated his spirit.

"Alright, alright," Matthias said with a laugh in his voice. "I expect to see you back here tomorrow. I'm going to overcharge you for your order!"

"Oh I'll be back here tomorrow," Egon said. "But Gustav is going to pay for my coffee!"

"I'll buy your coffee," Gustav said. "But you pay for my pastries."

Everyone at the table laughed. Matthias looked back and shared a moment of eye contact with Camilla. They shared a smile. For the first time in weeks, both of their smiles were genuine.

PART XI

"How can one live when life without football is nothing?"

—Unknown

atthias and Camilla were kissing as they walked through the door of their apartment. As they closed the door behind them, Camilla wrapped her arms around Matthias' broad shoulders. He held onto her waist and drew her close to him.

As their tongues touched, she could feel his heartbeat in excitement for her. She pulled away from the embrace and walked to the doorway of the bedroom. She pulled her dress off of her body and motioned for him to join her. He approached her and with one hand, held her body close to him and with the other, held one of her breasts in his hand. He kissed her again, slipping his tongue into her mouth. She began to walk back into the bedroom. They collapsed onto the bed. As they continued kissing, he ran his fingertips over her shoulders and down her arms. Their hands met, and their fingers interlaced. Each moment they kissed, they could feel their love grow stronger than before.

Outside, snow began to fall. The night was being watched over by the owl. The moon struggled to send the light being reflected from the sun down to the Earth below through the thick clouds.

Snowflakes gathered on their windowsill. As the couple held each other through the night, they could feel a slight chill in the air. Matthias pulled the comforter up over them as they watched the ceiling fan spin around. Both of them were dreaming with their eyes open.

"What are you thinking about?" he asked her.

"What our children will be named."

"I thought we already settled on Pedro if it was a boy."

"That is not going to happen," she said as she slapped his chest. They both laughed and he held her a little closer. "I'm cold, go get me some tea, darling."

He sat up and rubbed his lower back gently before getting out of bed. He walked into the kitchen without bothering to put on a robe. He filled the teapot with water, placed it on a burner, and tried to turn on the stove. As he did, he fumbled with the knob.

"This worked earlier," he thought to himself.

He heard the gas spout out and he stared at it for a moment. Then, he turned the knob again and the pilot caught the gas and a circle of flame appeared around the burner.

As he waited for the water to boil, he opened the bottle of whiskey they received as a gift from Andreas. He noticed that the cork was loose but he did not give it too much thought. He poured two glasses of whiskey. He noticed the color was a little different from other whiskeys that he was used to. He picked up the bottle and looked at the label closely.

"Product of Scotland" he read. "Maybe that explains the color."

He came back into the bedroom and handed Camilla one of the glasses.

"While we wait for the tea to boil," he said with a grin.

They touched the glasses together and took a sip.

"Oh, I almost forgot," Camilla took another sip of the whiskey and placed it on her nightstand. She pulled out the drawer and pulled out a magazine. "I wanted to show this to you."

She opened it up and pointed out a picture of mountains reminiscent of the Swiss Alps.

"Where is this," he asked.

"It's Wyoming," she said with a smile.

"It's what?"

"It's a state in America. It's where I want us to go on our honeymoon."

He took the magazine from her and he looked at the pictures. The snow-capped mountains, wide-open fields, the majestic elk. It looked like something out of another world to him. It seemed like a place reserved only for folklore. He smiled. He wanted to give Camilla whatever she wanted.

"You want to go to Wyoming instead of the south of France?"

"We can do both, can't we?"

He leaned in to kiss her and she leaned in to meet his kiss. The moment was interrupted by the sound of the teapot whistling.

He poured them both a cup and came back to the bedroom.

"What do you think it would be like in Wyoming?" he wondered.

"Obviously it will be snowing. The magazine says you can see herds of elk throughout the year."

"Are elk like reindeer?"

"They look like it from the pictures."

As they talked they laughed and held each other. They enjoyed daydreaming about what their honeymoon would be like. Talking about this magical land of unforeseen beauty.

Matthias gazed off into the shadows and took a deep breath. He imagined seeing the sunrise over the Tetons, seeing eagles soar overhead, butterflies flapping their wings over the flowers.

"Is that a butterfly on my feet," he wondered.

He reached for it and as his fingers stretched out, it flew away.

His eyes followed its path into the sky and over the mountains.

The peaks seemed so magisterial that he thought he could fly. He smiled as he saw the top of the peaks that see only the palace of God. As he gazed at the awful sight of the Grand Tetons he looked over at Camilla. He wanted to show her the peaks and valleys, the amazing sights that he was seeing.

"Why is she lying down?" he thought.

She was sprawled out on the mattress, lying face down. Her eyes were open, motionless.

He tried to get up to tap her shoulder. As he reached for her, he fell over next to her. As he lay next to her, his eyes began to close. His hand found her hand and there it stayed--forever.

PART XII

"Sometimes the idol doesn't fall all at once."

—Eduardo Galeano, *Soccer in Sun and Shadow*

January 23, 1939

Fog settled in over the city. It created an uncomfortable feeling for many people walking through the streets of Vienna. As the sun tried to break through the morning clouds, the fog clung to the atmosphere above the historic city. Columns of light from the sun shone down on the cobblestones that paved the streets.

Gustav Hartmann enjoyed seeing Matthias the previous evening. Neither he nor Egon had seen their friend for some time and they were happy to catch up with him. They were going to meet at the Cafe Sindelar and continue to catch up.

When Gustav arrived, he was surprised to find the shop still closed. Egon was not there yet. It was already 9 in the morning. Gustav peered through the windows, shielding his eyes from the morning sunlight as he tried to look inside.

"Is the place closed?" Egon said as he approached. Gustav was startled and looked over.

"No," he responded. "This is a bit odd. You would

think he'd be punctual."

"Well, we were all up late. Maybe he's hungover."

Gustav was more suspicious about why their friend's shop was not open. He ran his hand over his mustache and looked back at the glass door. He pushed his lips together and put his hands on his hips.

"I feel like something is wrong," he said after a moment.

"I'm sure he's fine. Come, I'm dying for a coffee."

They found another cafe nearby. Gustav was distracted. He could not shake his curiosity as to why Matthias did not show up to open his own cafe on a Monday morning.

"Egon," he said finally breaking the tension. "I think something might be wrong."

"With Matthias?"

"Yes. It's too strange."

"I'm sure he's just hungover. You saw how much he was drinking, didn't you?"

"Both you and I saw him hungover. He scored goals hungover."

"He's not as young as he used to be."

"Well, if he's so damn hungover then why didn't Camilla open up the shop?"

"If it's bothering you so much, why don't you call him?"

Gustav sat back in his chair and crossed his arms over his chest. He stared off into space for a moment and then got up from the table, marched over to the maitre d' station, and asked to use the phone.

He called Karl Sesta.

After a few minutes, he walked back to the table.

"What's going on?" Egon asked. Gustav did not sit back down.

"I just called Karl. He's going to meet us in front of the building."

K arl was already waiting at the building's front steps when they arrived. All three walked together up to Matthias' apartment. Karl knocked on the door.

"Matthias!" he shouted in between knocks.

After a moment, he knocked again. This time a little louder.

BANG BANG BANG

"Matthias! It's Karl! Please answer the door!"

BANG BANG BANG

Karl looked at Egon and Gustav.

"I'm going to find the Allrounder," Karl said.

As Karl started to walk away, Gustav lurched forward and threw all of his weight into the door. He did it again and then the wooden door tore in half. He reached through the hole and unlocked the door, opening it.

He stepped inside and saw an open bottle of whiskey sitting on the dining table. Suddenly, he found it hard to breathe and he began to cough. They all pulled out their handkerchiefs. They placed the cloth over their noses and mouths as they walked a little further into the apartment.

Then all three of the men stopped and stared. They lowered their hands from their faces. Their mouths were hanging open as they tried to make sense of what they were looking at. Camilla and Matthias, face down, naked in bed, completely motionless.

Karl reached for Gustav's shoulder, in an attempt to catch his balance.

"Ca..." Karl stammered as he tried to find the correct words. "Call the police."

Police and medical workers arrived. They carried the lifeless bodies of Camilla and Matthias out of the apartment. Karl, Gustav, and Egon waited in front of the apartment building. Tears were rolling down their cheeks. Karl stood, arms crossed across his chest. Gustav and Egon both sat on the steps.

Without warning, a man who was their friend,

colleague, and inspiration was gone. He was never coming back. They could not make sense of what had happened or why it happened. They all wondered if there was anything they could have done differently the night before to change what had happened. As they wept, all they could do was wonder why and how. Karl wondered what the last thing he said to Matthias was, he could not remember.

Inside the apartment, about a dozen police officers milled about. They combed through the bedroom, searching for anything suspicious. Jurgen Schrempf stood in the middle of the dining room. He was holding the bottle of whiskey from the dining room. He held the spout up to his nose and sniffed it. He turned around and saw a young officer, Stefan Schobesberger, in the kitchen. He was examining the oven. He walked past the young officer and to the kitchen sink. He then proceeded to pour the alcohol down the drain.

"Kriminalobersekretar Schrempf," Schobesberger said excitedly. "Look at this."

Schrempf dropped the now empty bottle into the bottom of the sink and walked over to the young officer. Schobesberger pointed out a series of puncture holes in the gas line. On the spigot, there was what looked like intentional tampering. The metal seemed slightly dented.

"Thank you, officer," Schrempf said unenthusiastically.

"I should get a photographer."

"No need. I'll make sure it is in the final report. Head back to headquarters and find out if there is any update concerning the autopsy."

"Yes, Kiminalobersekretar! Heil Hitler!"

He rushed out of the apartment and headed down the hallway. Schrempf looked more closely at the punctures on the gas line and shook his head.

Schobesberger ran past the three mourners and across the street. He was stopped by a young man wearing round glasses, a tan raincoat, and a black Fedora.

"Excuse me, sir," the stranger said. "I'm with the Krone. Phillip Dibbon. Can you tell me what happened?"

He was a reporter. The Krone was shorthand for Kronen Zeitung, one of the largest and most powerful newspapers in Vienna. Dibbon was a new, young, and eager journalist with the publication.

"Looks like a couple was killed," the officer responded, obviously forgetting the proper chain of command when dealing with the press. "Could've been gas poisoning."

Dibbon wrote in his notebook while the officer ran towards his car. The reporter approached Karl, whose head was hung low, his arms still across his chest.

"Excuse me," Dibbon said softly. "Aren't you Karl Sesta?"

"I am," he said through his tears.

"Did you know the people who lived here?"

"Oh yes. You did too. They got Sindi."

S chrempf!"

The bark from Max Uhrmann startled every one of the Gestapo officers within earshot. Jurgen Schrempf looked around and saw his superior officer standing under the archway.

"My office! Now!"

Uhrmann marched off and Schrempf stood up and rushed to follow Uhrmann into his office.

Once in the office, Schrempf stood unsure of what to say. Uhrmann picked up a copy of that day's Krone and slammed it on his desk and pointed at an article.

"Explanation, please!"

Schrempf leaned over the desk and picked up the newspaper tentatively. The headline, "Matthias Sindelar Dead!" Then he began to read the article written by someone he had not heard of, Phillip Dibbon. He skimmed all the particulars and then stared at the first sentence of the second paragraph: "Everything points towards this great man having become the victim of murder through poisoning."

After reading the sentence several times, Schrempf

looked up at Uhrmann. He had never seen his face so stern. It was almost like a stone.

"Well?"

The superior officer was speaking through his teeth.

"I have no idea why they would reach such a conclusion. I never saw a reporter at the apartment."

"Find out what this clown of a reporter is talking about! The last thing we need is the rumor mill going crazy! These Viennese can only do one thing well and that's spread gossip like a Jew spreads disease!"

Schrempf nodded his head and folded the newspaper.

"Why are you still standing there! Fix this!" Uhrmann ordered.

Phillip Dibbon was in love with his typewriter. The clinking and the clanking of the machine-driven solely by imagination, sweat, and perseverance inspired him to do what he did best, which was write. The typewriter sat on a desk in his bedroom. It was surrounded by notes and books and papers. He was trying to write a novel but had no idea what he should write about.

Phillip stared at his face in the mirror. He ran a comb through his thin brown hair. He was wondering if he should shave that morning. After running his fingers over the stubble, he decided that he would. He filled his sink with warm water and dropped his shaving brush into it. He splashed some of the water onto his face and then applied some pre-shave oil. Then, he pulled the brush from the sink and shook out the excess water. He then picked up his shaving soap and ran the brush's bristles over the soap creating a nice lather. Gently, he applied the newly created cream to his face. He picked up his safety razor and shaved away his whiskers.

While he watched his face become clean-shaven, he thought about his life up to this point. He thought about why he decided to become a journalist. He wanted to hone his craft as a writer. He never really thought he could be a hero of the Fourth Estate, like so many of his colleagues at the Krone. He just wanted to write.

Phillip Dibbon was born and raised in Vienna. Growing up, he was a lot shorter than most of the other kids in his class. That meant that he got picked on a lot. He was not an avid sportsman, but he enjoyed watching football with his father. Without many friends, he found friends of his own in the likes of Professor Pierre Aronnax, Dr. Griffin, Captain Nemo, and Uriah Heep.

As he grew up, adventure novels gave way to newspapers and he discovered an easy way to churn out a living by telling stories. The Krone offered him a job on the city desk. He was not sure how long he would really be working at the daily newspaper as he always felt that his true calling was to write a book of his own one day. He dreamed of writing a book that would inspire future storytellers who felt like they did not fit in with the social conventions of the day.

When he was done shaving, he put on his aftershave and patted his face dry with a towel. He put on his white button-down shirt and then his trousers. He pulled his suspenders over his shoulders and found his shoes. He sat in his bed as he put them on his feet. He looked back at his typewriter and sighed as he forced himself to leave for the office.

He walked into the newsroom on that Monday morning and heard nothing but the cacophony of a room full of typewriters clanging and banging while writing out that day's news. He found his way to his desk and sat down. It was a disorganized mess, covered in papers and notes. Dull pencils sat in a coffee cup. Before he was able to get comfortable and settled, his editor approached him.

"Dibbon," he said. "There was a break-in at Schwarz Pharmaceuticals. Go check it out."

"Right away, boss!"

Phillip hoped that he would be able to work on a follow up to the Sindelar story from the previous day. When he got the assignment to go to Matthias' apartment, he did not know whose apartment it was. He was only told that two people were found dead inside an apartment building.

But even though it was he who broke the story, there was another reporter who was assigned the follow-up. The crime beat was Phillip's beat after all, and it was a crime that he had to cover. He noticed that the editors at the Krone were becoming more interested in salacious stories, like dead couples in apartments or break-ins at businesses. Stories like these did not really interest him. He wanted to know who people actually were on the inside. He wanted to know who were the people passing and writing laws. But he was just a beat reporter who was always overruled in the newsroom.

"People don't want to read anymore," he was once told by his editor. "They just skim. Besides, we don't sell newspapers so they can read the news. We sell them newspapers so they can see the ads."

Phillip knew there was more to the story of the deaths of Matthias and Camilla. Even though the story was not his assignment anymore, he wanted to uncover the truth about it.

The coroner's office was cold and purposefully uninviting. Located beneath the Viennese Police station, Dr. Harald Quester sat behind a typewriter trying to write out a death certificate. He ran his fingers through his graying beard as he reviewed his notes before he continued typing. He was interrupted when the remains of Matthias and Camilla were brought in, their lifeless bodies were moved from the stretchers and placed atop an examination table.

"Two more for you, Doctor," the intern said. "They were found this morning."

"Thank you," was his reply.

Dr. Quester stood up from his desk, walked over to the sink, washed his hands, and put on his apron. He rubbed the lenses of his glasses on the cloth of the apron before putting them back on his face.

The science behind the post-mortem always fascinated the doctor. He was enthralled by it before he went to medical school and knew he always wanted to be a coroner. He felt like a detective, a Sherlock Holmes with a medical degree. Here he was, answering the one question that, in some cases, even the deceased did not always know the answer to--what caused this suspicious death? Why did this person die? Dr. Quester had the ability to figure it out and solve what some thought was unsolvable and he had been doing it for over twenty years.

He traced his fingertips over Matthias' neck, looking for any lumps or tumors. He did not find any. He then felt over the chest and abdomen. Then the groin area and over the thighs. He did the same to Camilla's corpse, repeating the digital examination.

He then picked up the police report and read it over. He then looked back at the bodies and placed the report down. He prepared the toe tags and walked back into his office. He picked up his phone and called his intern to join him.

Assistant Public Prosecutor for the City of Vienna, Arnold Drazan, did not think he was going to be assigned the Sindelar case. It was the talk of the office since the news broke. He was not expecting it as he was not senior enough in stature for such a case. Sindelar was a celebrity. Surely this case was one that the chief prosecutor would handle. Drazan was still young, he was in his early 20's, and inexperienced as a lawyer.

"New assignment," said the intern who walked into his office as he handed him a file.

"Thank you," Drazan responded. He put on his glasses and looked at the name on the file. "Sindelar."

His jaw dropped.

"They want me on this?" he said out loud.

The youthful attorney ran his hands through his blond hair and he took a deep breath as he opened the file. His eyebrows perked up as he read the words, "gas valve appeared intact."

He sat back in his chair and thought about all the different possibilities of why Sindelar died.

"Why would someone of Sindelar's stature commit suicide?"

There was no note. It was well known amongst the party officials that Sindelar had a dissident nature in him.

"But why would anyone kill himself just because they don't like the government?" he thought to himself. "And as a double suicide with his fiancee? Suicide should not be seen as the only possibility. Foul play must be investigated."

His suspicions grew. He thought someone had to be behind the death.

Dr. Harald Quester and his intern, Jorg Unterreiner, began the extensive examination of Matthias and Camilla. Jorg watched the doctor and took copious notes concerning the examination. He had served as Dr. Quester's intern for several months. He was underweight and always showed up for work clean-shaven. But his shoes were never shined. The leather was wrinkled and worn down.

"I'm inserting the syringe into the right arm of the deceased male. Withdrawing ten milliliters. Will check for oxygen levels, toxicity, and other irregularities."

Jorg wrote that down.

"Around the nostrils, the capillaries are exposed. Blood vessels in the eyes show as well, pupils are dilated. There is some bubbling around the lips and around the tonsils."

Jorg was scribbling furiously. He was trying to keep up with everything his mentor was finding.

"What does that mean?" the intern asked.

"Some sort of chemical reaction."

"Poisoning?"

"Perhaps," the doctor walked over to the sink to wash his hands. "However, we won't know for certain until the blood work comes back. Until then, we can only hypothesize. We do know that there are no signs of obvious physical trauma. No bruising, no cuts, or anything of the sort. This man and woman clearly died without putting up any kind of fight. Therefore, it is not unreasonable to hypothesize that they were poisoned, most likely by carbon monoxide."

Arnold Drazon was still at his desk, he had been there all night researching the life of Matthias Sindelar and questions for the coroner. He was unshaven and his hair was unkempt. His suit jacket hung on the back of his chair and his shirtsleeves were rolled up to his elbows. Half-eaten pastries were littered across his desk along with a cup of cold coffee.

His focus was broken when Max Uhrmann entered his office unannounced. The young lawyer looked up from his work and saw the Nazi officer, in full regalia, sitting himself down in the chair in front of Drazen's desk.

"When was the last time you took a shower?" Uhrmann asked matter of factly.

"I beg your pardon? Can I help you?"

"I know you're looking into the death of Matthias Sindelar and that of his live-in girlfriend, Camilla Castagnola."

"I am and may I ask, who are you?"

Uhrmann stood and walked over to the window, unlatched it, and opened it. "This room is begging for some fresh air. It will help you think better. I am Max Uhrmann and I answer to the Fuhrer."

Arnold leaned back in his chair and took a deep breath.

"I came here directly from Metropole," Uhrmann

continued, looking directly at the young attorney, allowing the light of the sun to silhouette him. "If you would prefer, we can continue this conversation there."

Arnold remained silent. He knew immediately the gravity of the situation that he was being threatened with. His shoulders sank slightly, trying hard to not show just how intimidated he actually was.

"I know that in your profession you are used to being the one to ask questions," Uhrmann said while he took his seat again, this time crossing his leg, resting his right ankle on his left knee. "But I would encourage you not to ask too many questions at this critical juncture. Now, I understand that you are looking into the death of Sindelar and Castagnola, is that correct?"

"I am."

"What have you found?"

Arnold looked at his notes, trying desperately to collect his thoughts. He took a deep breath through his nose and his fingers found a pencil to clutch onto. Even though it was not much, it gave him a minute sense of security, shielding him slightly from the menacing man before him.

"I have reason to believe that the deaths were not accidental," he said hesitantly. "I suspect something foul might be afoot."

Max nodded and straightened his posture, placing

both feet on the ground.

"You will tell your superiors that you found nothing," he responded. Arnold was taken aback. "You will also tell them that there is no reason to investigate further. The deaths were suicide."

Drazan struggled to find the words to respond to this demand. Max stood and began straightening his jacket.

"But why?" he finally said. "There was no note. No history of mental illness."

"There is no reason to investigate any further. You will tell your superiors that you agree with the coroner's findings that the death was suicide."

Arnold, now standing as well, quickly shuffled through his papers and found the coroner's report.

"But the coroner did not come to that conclusion yet. He has not even written a preliminary autopsy."

"It will say suicide. The case is closed. Are we understood? Or do you need more convincing? Because if you do, that can be easily arranged."

Arnold fell silent and sat back down.

"I understand."

"Good. Heil Hitler."

"Heil Hitler."

Max exited the office. Arnold closed his folder and looked out his window on the city.

D r. Harold Quester sat at his desk prepared to write his final report on the deaths of Matthias Sindelar and Camilla Castagnola. He lined up the template in his typewriter and began to type the words "PRELIMINARY AUTOPSY." He had not yet received the final results from the bloodwork he ordered but he was confident enough to begin the report. His experience taught him that he could anticipate certain results.

He continued typing:

"All results presented within this report are concurrent with the results of the beginnings of the investigation. Conclusive findings will be presented following results from blood work and a full and complete autopsy.

SUBJECT: SINDELAR, MATTHIAS

AGE: 35

HEIGHT: 175 CENTIMETERS

WEIGHT: 66 KILOS

HAIR: BLONDE

EYES: HAZEL

CAUSE OF DEATH:

Before he typed anything, he sat back in his chair and lifted a cigarette to his lips. He took a long drag and blew out the smoke.

"What a waste," he whispered to himself.

As he tapped out the ash in his ashtray, he was interrupted by Arnold Drazan who barged into the examination room. The doctor looked up surprised by the interruption. He stood and walked over to the doorway between his office and the examination room.

"Herr Drazan. To what do I owe this unexpected honor?"

"We need to discuss the deaths of Matthias Sindelar and Camilla Castagnola."

K arl Sesta stood in the middle of the sidewalk, in front of a newsstand, looking at the front page of the Krone. He was frozen in place. He could not believe what he was reading. Tears began to roll down his face.

"This can't be true," he said to himself.

The words making up the headline were simple and clear, "Matthias Sindelar's Death Ruled A Suicide."

"Impossible!"

His words began to grow slightly louder. He knew Matthias like a brother. He read the headline over and over again. He could not comprehend what he was reading. He simply could not read any further. The words on the page felt like daggers being plunged right into the heart of his soul. To read the next lines would be a herculean feat and he did not know if he had the strength to do so. In a way, continuing to read the story would force him to accept the fact that it was actually real.

The world was spinning around him. He walked over to the nearest park bench and sat down. He could not hear the world around him, he could only hear his heart beating. His head rested in his hand and he ran his fingers through his dark curly hair. His elbow rested on the armrest and his fingers clutched on his locks as if he were trying to pull his hair from his scalp. He needed to feel something to make sure he was not trapped in a nightmare. From his throat came a wail of emotional exhaustion.

"Why Sindi?" he pleaded.

He looked up and saw a cross atop a church steeple. He could not understand what kind of god, whether it was Jesus or Zeus or Shiva, would allow someone so beloved as Sindi to die unnaturally. Through his tears, he tried to find the strength to pray. He tried to make sense of the senseless.

After what seemed like an eternity, he picked up the newspaper and tried to read what was written.

"The findings are consistent with suicide by carbon monoxide poisoning," he read.

"Impossible," he said to himself as he read.

"There is reason to believe that Matthias and his

fiancee had a suicide pact," the article said.

After reading that line, he crumpled up the paper and threw it on the street. He closed his eyes shut tightly. His mouth fell open as he cried uncontrollably. He tried to catch his breath, but his emotions were making it hard for him to breathe. His heart was beating wildly.

It was the end of an era, not only marking the end of the Wunderteam, but also the end of a chapter in his life. For the remainder of his days, he would never see one of his best friends and confidants again. He wished for the ability to turn back time. He wanted to make up for all the times he did not show up at Walter's to play cards and smoke cigars. All the times he did not ask Matthias how he was. He felt like he had taken his friendship for granted.

From the church steeple, he looked down and saw the Nazi flag. His head began to nod back and forth. The symbol of a government he supported, he was now beginning to resent. He felt like he was truly alone. Because of the Nazi policies, Walter was in Switzerland. Now, Matthias was gone and he knew, deep down, the story he was being told about his death was a flat out lie.

Jurgen Schrempf had a small smile on his face as he sipped a cappuccino in the outdoor patio of a cafe. A folded up copy of the Krone sat on the table. He looked out at the square before him and just daydreamed about nothing in particular. Otto joined him, he sat down with a croissant. They were taking a break from investigating potential enemies of the state to enjoy a coffee.

"I think it's colder here than in Warsaw," Otto said.

"If I didn't get lucky with Sindelar, I think Uhrmann would've made sure that I got sent there," Jurgen replied.

"What do you mean, 'get lucky?'"

"I mean if he didn't drop dead. I no longer have to keep digging into that piece of shit's boring life."

Otto looked at him blankly. A million different thoughts were running through his head.

"Jurgi," Otto began before Jurgen raised his hand to stop him from saying anything further.

"The case is now closed, my friend." Jurgen raised his eyebrows and took another sip of coffee. "He's dead. It says right there in the newspaper that the fucker's dead. He killed himself. Suicide. He won't be haunting our corridors of power anymore."

Am I the only one who thinks it's odd that Sindelar killed himself?" Phillip asked in the afternoon editorial meeting. "I mean, he didn't even leave a note, don't you think that's strange? The police are the ones who told us that it was a suicide pact but they won't tell us how they came to these conclusions."

The news team would meet at least twice a day to go over that day's news and discuss how the stories would be covered. The gaggle of newsmen met in a windowless conference room, sitting around an oblong wooden table. The room was filled with cigarette smoke. Many men were drunk from drinking too much beer or scotch at their lunch. Phillip was merely hoping that he would be assigned a follow-up story about the Sindelar death.

"Do you really think you'll get anyone to tell us anything differently?" one of the reporters asked with a half-smile on his face.

"Have we asked?" A fair question from Phillip, unfortunately, it was one question that everyone in the room knew the answer to. The other journalists and editors in the room all looked at each other or looked at their notes.

"The report came directly from Metropole," the chief editor said. With that, it was a signal for Phillip to not ask any more questions.

The young reporter looked out the window and had a fleeting thought. At any other time, in any other country, the answer he would have received from his editor might have been different. Phillip might have been assigned a story questioning the report of Matthias' and

Camilla's deaths. But in 1939 Vienna, one did not question the information given from those in authority.

Journalists were the last people expected to question authority. The profession became a cursed one. Adolf Hitler and other high ranking Nazis constantly accused reporters of lying and of helping the enemy. Phillip knew he was not in a position to ruffle any feathers with either his employer or with his nation.

Walter Nausch smoked a pipe in his living room while he read a book. His wife Margot was preparing their lunch. They were slowly settling into their life in Zurich. It was not easy for them even though they were living in a German neighborhood. The couple had trouble settling. They did not have a group of friends. They were far away from family. It was not home and it would take some time before they felt like they were home.

As he puffed on his pipe, he rubbed his leg. His muscles ached, longing to run on the pitch again. His foot missed the feel of the ball as he kicked it. He missed his glory days of youth.

There was a knock on the door. Walter got up from his chair and walked to the door. When he opened the door, he saw a messenger.

"Herr Walter Nausch?" the young man said.

"Ya."

"Telegram for you, sir."

Walter was handed a piece of paper and the young man walked off. As Walter tried to open the telegram while closing the door, Margot came into the living room holding a pot of tea. She saw her husband staring at the telegram.

"What is it?" she asked.

Walter's head started shaking from side to side. Tears began to form in his eyes.

"Darling?" she begged, wanting him to talk to her. "What is it?"

"They got Sindi," he finally said. "I can't. I can't."

He held out his hand to show her the note. She grabbed hold of it and quickly looked at it.

"SINDI AND CAMILLA DIED MONDAY MORNING. THEY SAY IT WAS SUICIDE. WANTED TO LET YOU KNOW. - KARL"

Frantically, Margot held her husband and held him. They both cried in each other's arms.

Phillip sat down for lunch at a park bench. He pulled out his notebook and began to go over his notes for the story he was going to write. He was not assigned the Sildelar follow up. Instead, he was assigned a piece about elderly women who were members of a quilting club.

As he sank his teeth into a brat he just purchased, its oily juices spilled out onto his chin, he panicked as he looked for a napkin.

"Don't I know you?"

Phillip looked up at who was asking him the question. He saw Karl Sesta standing in front of him. Phillip recognized him as the man from a few days before.

"Karl?" Phillip patted away the mess from his chin.

"You're that reporter, right?"

"Yes, Phillip Dibbon." A part of Phillip was excited because he was hoping that he could turn this random chance meeting into a new story. "Would you like to join me?"

"Thank you." Karl sat and pulled up his collar to keep warm. "Phillip, can I ask you a question?"

"Of course."

"What did you think of his last match?"

"The Anschluss match?"

"Yes."

"It was an exciting game, particularly at the end."

"What did you think of the result?"

"I thought it could've been 5 nil. Sindi had a number of good chances."

With that, Karl smiled.

"I was with him the day before he died. I practically lived with the man during our playing days. I remember I once asked him what it was about football that he loved so much. Do you know what he told me? He told me that it was one of the few games where David could truly beat Goliath. Sometimes, you get lucky and strike Goliath between the eyes with a stone. Other times, you have to break him down, bit by bit until Goliath can no longer stand. There is no way he killed himself. Why would they say it was a suicide? I just don't understand it at all. Why would they do that to us?" Karl looked over and saw the reporter writing shorthand in his notebook. A sudden wave of panic came over him. He was worried about saying too much or the wrong people using his suspicions against him. "Please put that away. I'm sorry, but I should be going now."

"Wait, I was just..."

"It's ok, son. I don't want to take up any more of your time. Enjoy your lunch."

Karl turned, straightened out his Fedora, and walked away. Phillip was too stunned to say anything more. He wrapped the rest of his brat in the paper bag he purchased it in and decided to head back to the newsroom. He kept replaying the interaction he had with Karl over and over in his head.

When he got back to his desk, he approached another journalist, Boris, who was working on a story. As he was typing, he had a pencil firmly between his teeth.

"Got a moment," Phillip asked.

"Sure," Boris looked up from his typewriter at the young journalist. He took the pencil out of his mouth and spun it between his fingers.

"There's something that I'm a bit hung up on concerning the Sindelar death."

"What's that?"

"I just ran into someone talking about it," Phillip did not want to say who he met in case he had a big story to pitch. "And of course he did not believe that he actually committed suicide."

"What's your question, Dibby?"

"Well, he said, 'Why would they do that to us?' Not, 'Why did he do that to us?' But, 'Why did THEY do that to us?' What do you think he was meaning?"

"German law. People of note or celebrity who commit suicide are not allowed to receive an official state funeral."

"Really? I didn't know that."

"He'll be buried, but basically only close friends and family will be invited."

Phillip nodded and thanked Boris. He walked back to his desk and sat down. He was lost in thought.

"Why would the Nazis not want to give Matthias a state funeral?" he thought to himself.

He quickly knocked out his story about the quilting club and left work.

As he was walking home, a young man bumped into him. As Phillip caught his balance, he was surprised to find a piece of paper in the middle of his chest. He spun around to see if he could spot the person who bumped into him but he was lost in the crowd. He looked at the piece of paper and saw a picture of Matthias' face on it. Above it the words: "The Nazis wanted him dead." On the bottom of the picture, three downward facing arrows pointing to the left, the symbol of the Iron Front, a Nazi-resistance group. Then the words, "Join O5."

Phillip looked at this quizzically. His suspicions were beginning to get the best of him. He folded up the paper and hid it in his hat. This was something he did not want to lose.

Throughout the night, Phillip kept looking at the flyer. He could not sleep. He was unfamiliar with what the three arrows were or what O5 was. With all of his suspicions he was contemplating from the day before, he was now enthralled with the idea of finding out the truth.

He tried to lie down in bed to get a little bit of sleep, but he could barely keep his eyes closed. His mind kept racing with so many different thoughts. He glanced out the window and saw a shadow scurry from one side of the street to the other. He looked more closely and saw that it was a rat sneaking into the sewers.

Phillip took a deep breath and sat down at his typewriter. He started to write out some of his thoughts about what happened the day before. He was rambling at first, but he knew that after at least a page or two, he would begin to make sense of it all.

Egon Ulbrich and Gustav Hartmann wanted to meet with Karl Sesta. The pair felt it was a travesty that the public would not be able to publicly mourn the death of Matthias Sindelar. To them, he was more than just a great athlete, he was a cultural icon. They wanted to do something to make it happen and hoped they could convince Karl to help them. Unfortunately, Matthias' former teammate was anything but receptive.

"Why would you want to do something like that," Karl argued.

"Do you honestly believe that he committed suicide?" Gustav asked.

"That's what they say! They sent investigators."

"The law says that people who committed suicide can not be given a state funeral," Egon said.

"Makes sense, don't you think? Why would anyone want to honor a man who killed himself?"

Gustav and Egon both looked at each other mournfully. Egon stood and crossed his arms. He walked over to the window and gazed outside. He took a deep breath and rubbed his hand over his cheek, feeling the little bit of stubble growing in.

"Have you heard of Hans Henninger?" Egon asked.

"The actor?"

"Yes. The Nazis say he killed himself."

"I know," Karl said in a terse tone. "I remember reading about it."

"Do you know why he killed himself?" Egon asked softly.

"He was a fairy, wasn't he?"

"The story they told us is that the Gestapo was coming to arrest him, and while they were knocking on the door, he blew his brains out."

"Does this story have a point?" Karl asked looking at Gustav. "What does this have to do with Matthias or why we're having this conversation?"

"But they did not just want his body in a prison camp," Egon said raising his voice. "They wanted his voice silenced too. Since they couldn't have Hans Henninger, they arrested his agent, his manager, directors, and other actors who worked with him too and accused them of being fairies as well!"

"But Matthias wasn't a homo!"

"In the eyes of Berlin, he was an enemy of the state!" Egon shouted. He stood and looked Karl directly in the eye. "In the eyes of Berlin, Matthias might as well had been a homo, or a communist or a Jew."

The room fell into a tense and uncomfortable silence.

"You know deep down that he would not have committed suicide," Egon continued. "We need to do something. If we don't, who knows what can happen."

"What are you suggesting that we do?" Karl asked in a dismissive tone.

"We need to figure out how to get the death certificate changed so we can have a proper funeral for him. One that he deserves," Gustav said.

"And what good would that do?"

"The same way the Nazis arrested Henninger's agent and co-stars," Gustav replied, "the Nazis could arrest Matthias' teammates for compliance in his dissident behavior."

"You're not serious," Karl chuckled at the suggestion.

"Or they could arrest everyone who cheered at him scoring that goal against Germany," Egon said. Karl raised an eyebrow and glared at him. "I seem to remember, Karl, that you scored the second goal in that game. The one that ensured an Austria victory."

Karl's body language immediately changed. His face began to show concern and the muscles in his shoulder tensed.

"Alright," he said. "I'm listening."

"There are people who are already trying to martyr Matthias," Egon said.

Gustav pulled out a piece of paper, identical to the one Phillip received. He laid it out on the coffee table.

"Someone slipped this into my pants pocket the other day," Gustav said softly.

"The resistance is using his name?" Karl asked.

"We're worried that if we don't get the death certificate changed, that the Nazis will use the words of the resistance against all of us."

"What on Earth are you talking about, Egon?" Karl shouted back.

"It's not enough to plead your innocence in a Nazi court," Egon pleaded. "In their eyes, we'd be guilty because of our association with Sindi. The possibility of being accused of treason or conspiracy or something of that nature is seriously real. We don't want to wind up in a prison camp. We are living in times of extremes and the Gestapo will do whatever they have to in order to hold onto control."

Karl sat back and took in what he was hearing. They both knew that Karl was not sympathetic to the resistance but he did desire to live a peaceful life. "And how will reclaiming his memory, as you put it, help us in this situation?"

"We have to try something. If the resistance holds onto Matthias' story, we could all become implicated in their cause by association."

"You think that we'll die either way?" Karl finally said.

"If we do nothing, if we do not allow the public to say goodbye, we very easily could die. The resistance will continue to use his name and try and martyr him. Then all of us might as well be wearing Eichmann's necktie. We seriously could be facing martial law and all of us will be considered guilty by the Nazis."

"I don't understand your reasoning."

"Karl, listen. Maybe the Nazis can make the trains run on time, but they will use a grenade to kill an ant."

"And that's why they rule Germany!" Karl's face turned red with frustration. "That's why Austria is now Germany! People don't want to live around filth. They want clean streets and neighbors they can trust!"

"That's why the Nazis will ultimately lose," Egon spoke softly. "Goliath was the most feared soldier of all. He crushed everyone and everything in his path. But he was defeated by a boy. He was defeated because of patience and cunning."

Karl turned his head. His face slowly began to regain its color.

"I could turn you in for what you just said."

"I know. But I trust you."

Karl buried his face in his hands. He breathed deeply.

"But many people are buying the official story about Matthias," he said. "It was in the newspaper, for crying out loud!"

"It is in the newspaper," Egon said.

"Newspapers are just the mouthpiece of the government," Gustav said.

"Wait a second," Egon said. "You're giving me an idea."

"What?" Gustav said.

"What about a reporter," he began. "We need to reach a reporter."

"A reporter?" Gustav asked.

"Like the one who came by Matthias' apartment."

"Why that kid, Egon?" Gustav asked. "Don't you know a lot of people who work for the papers?"

"Those are all sports reporters. They wouldn't understand what we're trying to do. We can use that reporter as cover to help us reach the coroner. Then he'll get a new official story printed."

"You'd be able to trust him," Karl said to the surprise of both Egon and Gustav. They both looked at Karl.

"Why do you say that?" Egon asked.

"I bumped into him earlier. I asked him about the Anschluss match. He said that he was surprised Matthias didn't score more goals."

Both Egon and Gustav slowly began to smile.

Across the different cafes, on street corners, and in restaurants across Vienna, people were talking about the death of the great Matthias Sindelar. Everyone had a different theory about why he died.

"He was killed because he was a secret Jew," was one theory spouted by some people.

"He killed himself! He was no hero! His footballing should be forgotten!" was something else many people said.

"Camilla was actually a prostitute and her pimp killed both of them!" That unfounded conspiracy theory was extremely popular amongst many of the people who craved the more salacious kinds of stories.

These rumors and speculations started to make their way into the lobby of the Metropole. People came into the office, off the street, offering the receptionists "proof" of who actually killed Matthias.

"I have a photo of a man in a black Fedora and a gray scarf going into Matthias' building," one person who came in said.

"Thank you, please let me have the photo," the receptionist replied.

"I smelled gas in my apartment and I think the man who killed Matthias is also trying to kill me!" another concerned citizen reported.

"Please write your address down on this paper and I'll have someone look into it."

"My husband wasn't home the night Matthias Sindelar died! He could have done it! You must investigate!" was another report someone made.

After some time, the receptionists in the Metropole could not deal with the myriad of unsubstantiated conspiracy theories and wild leads any longer. They were being bombarded by them daily. Finally, their complaints reached the ear of Max Uhrmann. His office had more important things to do than chase down leads with ideas conjured up out of thin air. As far he was concerned, the Sindelar case was closed.

"There are enemies in our midst who are trying to memorialize this dead footballer," Uhrmann said in a meeting with his subordinates. Jurgen Schrempf sat and listened in earnest. "Sindelar was unfriendly to the Reich, we know that based on how he behaved in the soccer match which celebrated Osterreich's union with Greater Germany. We know this based on his behavior after the match. He listened to American Negro music. He served Jews in the cafe he purchased from a Jew, and according to the investigative work from Kriminalobersekretar Jurgen Schrempf, we learned that he overpaid for that cafe. And he paid for it in cash."

Uhrmann paused and looked at his Gestapo officers in the eye.

"Gentlemen, this is not someone who should be martyred. This is a man who should be forgotten. We need to find out who is idolizing this dissident, and make sure they never move forward with their plans. It appears that the largest of this group is O5, then New Free Austria, Helfenberg and there are several others. We need to smoke out these rats and make sure their filth does not infect our nation any further. They are our enemy."

Max sat in the back of his Mercedes limousine, exhausted from his long day. All he could think about was going home as his driver chauffeured him through Vienna from the Metro. It was late, his wife would have to reheat his dinner. He hated driving almost as much as he hated being in the city he was assigned to. He told himself, and to anyone who asked, that not driving himself allowed him to focus his energy more closely on the task at hand, eliminating from the Third Reich all of its enemies.

"Stop!" he shouted as they passed St. Stephen's Cathedral. He saw a young man, maybe twenty years old drawing something on the side of the building. Max quickly got out of the car and chased after him. "You there! Stop!"

The young man ran off, into the shadows of the alleyway. Max couldn't keep up. He stopped running, knowing he wasn't going to be able to catch him as he tried to catch his breath. He grabbed for his emergency whistle to summon any police within earshot. He held it to his lips but he did not blow it. Instead, he stared at the graffiti the young man drew on the side of the church. He saw, written in chalk, thee arrows pointed down and to the left and one letter and one number: "O5".

Phillip sat at the same park bench, eating another lunch by himself. He was really beginning to hate his job. He opened up his notebook and began to jot down ideas for how he was going to write the story he was assigned that day.

"Fancy seeing you again," he heard. Phillip looked up and saw a familiar face.

"Karl," he said with a smile.

"May I join you?"

"Please." Phillip scooted over on the bench, making more room for the football star. "I must say, I honestly didn't think I'd see you again."

"Well, I'm glad I found you." Karl turned to face the reporter. "I need your help with something."

Phillip squinted his eyes as he was confused by what Karl had said. Why would Karl Sesta, the sporting hero, a man who he only met twice need his help?

"What do you mean?" Phillip asked.

"I don't want to discuss it now, but meet me at this address this evening. Seven pm. My friends and I have something we need to discuss with you." Karl took a pen from his pocket and wrote an address down in Phillip's notebook. "I hope to see you."

Then, he got up and walked away.

Karl and Gustav were sitting in Egon's apartment, listening to the grandfather clock in the living room tick away the seconds of the evening. It was 7:05 and with each tick and each sip of beer, Karl grew more uneasy.

"I don't think he's going to show up," Karl said.

"He'll be here," Egon said in an effort to reassure his friend. "You wrote down my address correctly, didn't you?"

"Of course I did." Karl got up and walked to the window. He could not see much of the outside world but the exercise calmed his nerves.

"Gentlemen," Gustav said. "What if he went to the Gestapo?"

Karl turned and looked at Egon. Karl lowered his arms and looked at Gustav. They all both took a deep breath as they realized that they had not considered that possibility. What if the reporter was only telling Walter what he wanted to hear when he asked about the Anschluss match? What if someone was spying on them in the park and got his address? A thousand other what-ifs ran through everyone's head in that split second.

"I trust Karl's instinct," Egon said. He turned and looked at Karl directly in the eye. "Your word is more trustworthy to me than anything else right now."

At that moment, they heard a knock on the door. They all gave each other looks of nervousness which quickly became looks of confidence. Egon went to the door and opened it. He saw Phillip standing in the hallway and only Phillip. He had his dark-colored overcoat on and he was holding his hat in front of his chest. A small smile crept over his face.

"Karl Sesta told me to come here," he said sheepishly.

"I remember you," Egon said. "From the day Matthias died. Come in."

Phillip walked in and nodded hello to the other two men in the room. Karl moved from the window to a winged chair and sat down. Phillip followed suit and sat on the couch across from the chair. He still did not know why he was invited to the apartment. He was confused as he looked around the living room. He saw a painting hanging on the wall. It was of the Wunderteam, painted by Paul Meissner. It showed the team wearing white kits and black shorts. In the foreground, couch Hugo Meisl. In the middle, running onto the field with his teammates was Matthias Sindelar. He was the captain, the centerpiece but he was one of many encompassing the entire team.

"Do you want a beer?" Egon asked.

"I'm fine," Phillip responded. "Thank you."

The three men looked around at each other,

wondering how to start the conversation.

"We, well," Egon began hesitantly before sighing and losing his words.

"Egon," Karl said interjecting. "This was your idea, so just say it."

Phillip looked baffled as he looked at the faces of both men.

"Ok," Egon said before taking a sip of beer. "There are concerns about the official report regarding Matthias' passing."

"I have questions about it too," Phillip said.

"It just seems so unlike him," Gustav said. "To commit suicide."

"We need to allow Vienna to say goodbye to him," Egon said.

"How does this concern me?" Phillip asked.

"You're aware of the law on the books about people who commit suicide?" Egon asked.

"I am," Phillip said. "But I don't know what you want me to do."

"We feel it's imperative to allow everyone to take part in owning his memory," Karl said.

"What do you mean?" Phillip asked.

Egon explained their concerns about how rumors and gossip could spread through the streets if the official cause of death is really suicide. The Nazi opposition groups across Vienna and Austria might try to martyr him and say that he killed himself because he could not stand the thought of living under Hitler any longer or that the Nazis killed him because of his past efforts to resist the Third Reich.

"What do you want me to do though?" Phillip pleaded. "I can guarantee you that my editors will not allow me to challenge the official story."

"We're not really looking for coverage in your paper, Phillip," Egon interjected. "The point is, we don't want anyone thinking anything suspicious. We want to stay alive, we want to live as much of a peaceful life as possible. But if we don't allow a state funeral, if we don't quell the rumors, we very well could be looking at martial law. The possibility is real. We don't want to wind up in a prison camp."

"I don't understand," Phillip said. "How can we have martial law if Matthias does not have a funeral."

"Martial law is the Nazis' answer to anything and everything," Gustav said. "The resistance is trying to use Matthias for their own benefit. If enough people believe that he died accidentally, we can allow this fascist Goliath to fall over itself."

"We need you to help us get in contact with the coroner," Egon explained. "We just need to change the death certificate."

Phillip was convinced. He felt that in some way, he could help. Unfortunately, he did not know anyone inside the morgue, but he did know someone who could connect him with the correct people. An old friend of his from primary school, Renata, was studying to become a nurse.

"It has been a long time," she said when he called her. "I'm surprised to hear from you actually."

After some small talk, he told her that he was working on a story and he was hoping that she could help him out.

"I need to speak with someone who does autopsies," he explained.

"I do know someone who works in the morgue actually. Jorg Unterreiner. He's another intern and he's studying to become a coroner."

"Oh, fantastic! He'd be perfect!"

"I'll call him."

The next day, he met Renata at the hospital and she walked him to the morgue. They found Jorg with his feet up on the table reading a newspaper while eating an apple.

"Renata!" Jörg was surprised to see her. He did have a small crush on her. "I forgot that I was meeting your friend today."

"I don't want to interrupt you," she said.

"No, I was, I was, you must be Phillip." Jorg held out his hand.

"Yes," the two men shook hands. "It's a pleasure to meet you."

"I'll let you two do what you need," Renata said. "I'll talk to you later, Jorg."

Renata left the morgue. Jorg threw the rest of his apple away. Then he quickly looked for a napkin and quickly cleaned his hands.

"So, how do you know Renata?" he asked, obviously sizing up any potential competition for her hand.

"We grew up together." Phillip looked at Jorg and could tell he was reading him. "We're old friends."

Jorg nodded and sat down.

"What's this story you're working on?"

"It's a follow up to Sindelar."

"Sindelar? Isn't that story done?"

"I'm hoping to get a look at his autopsy results."

"Why do you need to see that?"

"There are some questions that only your official report can answer."

"You do know that I'm just an intern. Your request has to go through proper channels. You'll need to speak with my superior."

"Time, unfortunately, is of the essence. Some

people are not convinced with what they are reading in the newspapers."

"It's funny what people believe and what people choose to believe." Jorg spun around in his chair and moved his head to the side to crack his neck. "What do you know about the Jewish resettlements?"

"The what?"

"The Jewish resettlements. What do you know about it?"

"Just that the Jews were being relocated. Why?"

"Do you think they are really being relocated?"

"I doubt they are happy."

Jorg looked at Phillip closely. He studied his eyes. He did not see hate, he saw compassion.

"But?"

"But what?"

"Is their relocation good for the Reich?"

The men stared at each other more. Jorg was trying to look into Phillip's soul.

"I don't know how it could be."

Jorg smiled and reached into his pocket and pulled out his wallet.

"I had a friend growing up. His name was Saul. A few months ago, I was supposed to have breakfast with him. When he didn't show up, I went to his apartment and found him in the bathtub. His wrists were slit. He was dead. Sitting on the floor of the bathroom was this note." Jorg pulled out of his wallet a white piece of paper with bloodstains on it. "The Nazis sent this to every Jewish home after that night in November."

Phillip took the paper from Jorg and looked at it closely. It was an official order. It said that all Jews had to turn their house keys over to German authorities, cancel all leases, and pack only what they could carry before reporting to the labor department to be sent to a work camp.

"I carry that note with me everywhere," Jorg said.

Phillip looked at the young doctor in training and nodded gently.

"Do you want me to show this to my editors?"

He handed the note back to Jorg who folded it back up and put it in his wallet.

"Your paper will never report it."

Phillip knew that he was right. The Krone had steered away from reporting anything controversial. The official line would be the one his editors would be fed from the Party, Jews were simply being moved and resettled in the East. If they questioned further, then they risk the ability of the paper to even function. But Phillip knew that he still had a role to play, even though he was no longer allowed to play it in the current climate.

"So what would you like me to do?"

"You want me to show you the autopsy report, right?"

"Yes."

"Well, you're a writer. Write this story for me, I'll make sure that it gets out and people can learn about what is really going on in this country."

"Do you have a printing press in your home?"

Jorg smiled.

"No," he said with a chuckle. "But I know the right people."

Phillip gave Jorg a long stare.

"Are you part of the resistance?"

"If you want the autopsy report, meet me tonight at 9. St. Stephen's." Jorg walked over to the door of the morgue and opened it. "It was a pleasure meeting you and good luck with your article!"

Philip walked up to him and looked him deep in the eye.

"How do you know I won't show up with Gestapo?" Phillip whispered.

"You would not have asked that if you would be."

S t. Stephen's Square is one of the dearest cultural centerpieces of Vienna. Sitting directly in front of the grand, Medieval cathedral, which is its namesake, the Square is a popular shopping center and a popular gathering spot. Covered in cobblestones, people walk freely, enjoy coffee and pastries in front of their favorite cafes or they sit on the steps of the Cathedral and read.

Earlier in the day, workers washed off an anti-Nazi graffito from the side of the Cathedral. But shortly after the sunset, someone else defaced the wall again with a similar design.

Sitting on the steps of the church, Philipp was waiting for Jorg to show up. He was shivering under his jacket and scarf. His hands, in gloves, were thrust deep in his jacket pockets. As he tried to keep warm, he wondered why he was waiting. He believed the hypothesis of Egon, Gustav, and Karl. He believed that the Nazis could do something awful to everyone if the resistance tried to turn Matthias into a martyr, even if he actually was one.

"But why do I have to risk my neck for them?" he thought to himself. If he gets caught, he will be killed.

He looked up at one of the spires and saw the moon in a crescent shape fit perfectly into the upper right quadrant of the cross. It hypnotized him for a moment.

"Are you Dibbon?" he heard from the shadows. He turned his head to see where it was coming from

"Jorg?" he asked in bewilderment.

"He's in here. Come with me."

"Where? Who are you?"

"In here, let's go. Now."

The young man led the reporter around the corner and knocked on a door on the side of the church. It was the entranceway where only the priests and nuns could enter. His knock was in a staccato rhythm, some kind of secret code.

A young priest opened the door. He looked around quickly and let them inside. Jorg motioned to Phillip to follow him into the church. They went down some brick steps and into what looked like a wine cellar. About a dozen people, most of them young university-age people, were in the room. When they saw Philipp enter, some people looked concerned as they did not recognize him.

Written in chalk on the brick wall were the letters AEIOU. On a chalkboard, someone wrote, "Being a person is not a crime." On the pillars, "O5" and the now-familiar three arrows representing the Iron Front. Philipp looked at them and knew he was in the presence of a resistance group. He gave everyone a slight but reassuring smile.

"Have a seat," Jorg said as he motioned to a chair near the back of the room.

He sat down in the back and looked around. He thought he was going to get information about Sindelar, but now he found himself in the center of a church and what looked like a secret prayer meeting.

"Who's he?" someone asked.

Jorg sat on a windowsill in front of everyone.

"He's with me," he responded. "Now listen. We know the Gestapo are everywhere. They have ears and spies in every nook and cranny of this city. Our friends and neighbors are being rounded up and sent to their deaths for no other reason than being who God made them. We need to remain vigilant. The rest of the world has decided that we don't matter. The British and the French have decided that we can all die at the hands of this tyranny. The Americans are asleep. The Italians are no longer our friends. We have to fight the Nazis ourselves. We don't have guns, but we have this!"

He held up a stack of papers.

"In these documents is proof that the Nazis are covering up the true cause of Matthias Sindelar's death!"

Everyone in the room sat up straight as they listened. Phillip focused a little more closely.

"I know, for a fact, that the investigation, and the autopsy, was ended by the orders of the Gestapo."

He looked around the room and made sure everyone was listening.

"Look for yourselves," he continued. "The findings of the autopsy were not fully recorded. Because we had to stop what we were doing because the German bastards were scared about what we would find!"

He threw the papers on a table nearby, exposing

the findings of the autopsy for Phillip's view. He got up and walked over to look at them. He looked closely and saw that the official autopsy had been cut short. The conclusive findings were not entered in the record.

"I can guarantee you that if Matthias were alive today, he would be sitting here amongst you right now to fight these fascist sons of bitches," Jorg said enthusiastically. This made Philipp's ears pick up. He remembered what Walter had said to him, about how someone was going to use Matthias' name in an attempt to turn him into a martyr.

"The people of Austria have to know the truth about what's going on! The truth is our only weapon right now! Now listen, right now, each and every one of us is committing treason. If we are caught, we will surely be killed. But remember, together as a group, as one, we are on the right side of history. The history books probably won't remember our names. But O5 will be a name no Austrian ever forgets."

One of the attendees, Stephen Murg, fresh out of his teens, stood.

"Jorg, you are right," Murg said. "But I fear you are forgetting that the Nazis only know one language! The language of fear and intimidation! We need to be as vigilant as we can!"

"If we are not careful, there will be no O5 left," Jörg

warned. "We need to tread lightly otherwise they will win."

The meeting went on for about an hour. The attendees heard Jorg speak on the importance of standing up to tyranny, what he planned on doing about it, and the importance of the invisibility of their cause.

As the meeting wound down, Philip moved to the back of the room. The attendees grabbed the leaflets from Jorg and some shoved them into their pants, others inside their hats, and others down their shoes or boots.

Once everyone left, Phillip approached Jorg.

"Nice speech," he said to Jorg.

"Did you get what you needed regarding the autopsy?"

"I think so. But I need to know something else."

"What's that?"

Philipp pointed to the chalk graffiti of the vowels and O5.

"What's that mean?"

"O5 is the name of our group. It means 'O' and 'E.' 'O' for Oesterreich and the five is because 'E' is the fifth letter of the alphabet."

"And the vowels?"

"Austria erit in orbe ultima," Austria will last

forever. It was the slogan of Friedreich III, Emperor of Austria in the Fifteenth Century. Jorg patted Philipp on the shoulder, motioning that they should go.

As they left, the young priest stopped the pair. He handed Jorg a gold coin. On one side was an image of the crucifixion. One the other, the words, "Resistentia ad tyrannide est, obedientia erga Deum."

"What is this?" Jorg asked as he looked at the gift.

"It says," the priest began, "'Resistance to tyranny is obedience to God.'"

Stephen Murg, the young man from the meeting, was on his way home when he spotted a police vehicle parked about a block up from where he was standing. Looking around, he didn't see anyone nearby. He reached into his pocket and found a piece of white chalk. Feeling emboldened by his perceived privacy and anonymity, he approached the vehicle.

With the chalk between his fingers, he crouched down, looked around again, and began to write "AEIOU" and "O5" all around the car's front driver's side tire. He started to laugh at himself for his luck at being able to graffiti a police car. He then reached out his leg to move down the car length to do the same to the rear tire.

"Can I help you?" the bold voice caused him to

freeze. Stephen looked over his shoulder and saw two police officers standing over him.

W hat is O5?" Jurgen yelled before punching Stephen in the face. The young man was tied to a chair in a windowless room that smelled like mold and mildew. His face was covered in a disgusting combination of sweat, blood, and drool. He had been there, tied up, and taking a beating for well over three hours.

"We just want answers," Otto yelled from the other side of the room.

Panting for breath, his eyes begging for mercy, the young man licked his lips and tasted his own blood. He closed his eyes and found his resolve. He looked up at his torturer and a taunting smile emerged on his face.

"O5?" Stephen said slowly as he breathed heavily. "It's where Mickey Mouse lives."

Jurgen pulled out his gun and pistol-whipped him with all his might. The force was so great, both Stephen and the chair he was tied to fell over onto the floor. He was now unconscious. A small pool of blood formed around his head.

"Bastard," the Gestapo agent said as he holstered his weapon. He walked to the other side of the interrogation room, picked up a rag, and wiped his hands.

"A little enthusiastic, Jurgi?" Otto asked with dripping sarcasm.

"He'll break sooner or later," he responded while he tossed the rag onto the floor. "Everyone does."

Otto crossed his arms and looked at the dirty floor. He stepped over the now unconscious young prisoner and walked towards his partner very slowly.

"Jurgi," he said sternly. "If he's dead, he won't be able to talk."

"If he's dead, that's one less Jew-lover in the world. So what's the problem?"

Otto raised his eyebrows and looked behind him at Stephen.

"We should at least make an attempt to get information out of him before we kill him, don't you think?"

Jurgen spit onto the floor and stared at Otto.

"He'll talk."

The temperature outside was near zero. Karl was sitting at a table at the Ring with Egon and Gustov. They each were sipping on a cup of coffee, in silence, as they waited for Phillip to arrive.

He finally did. He entered the cafe tentatively. Ever

since the meeting, he was becoming increasingly paranoid. But he felt compelled by the cause of allowing the death of Sindelar to be taken away from the hands of the Nazis. He felt like he was now part of something greater than himself. Before he met Karl, Egon, and Gustov, he had no idea that the death of an athlete, no matter how popular, could be turned into a revolutionary cause. But now, here he was, in the throes of a revolution. In his pocket was a coin to remind him of his motivation going forward. Every time he put his hands in his pockets, he felt the medallion. He ran his fingertips over the grooves and felt the letters. It served as a constant reminder, "Resistance to tyranny is obedience to God."

"Herr Sesta," he said as he approached the table. Karl turned around and saw the young journalist standing behind him.

"Herr Dibbon," he responded. "I'm glad you're here."

The other men stood up. At first, Phillip thought they were both standing to shake his hand.

"We should take a walk," Karl insisted. They wanted to talk outside because they were concerned about Gestapo spies and eavesdroppers.

As they went outside, Phillip took note of each of the three men taking their scarves and placing them over their faces, making sure they covered their mouths.

"I've seen the fliers and leaflets talking about Sindi," Karl said. "The rumors about the Nazis covering up his death are growing."

"Have you been in contact with the coroner?" Egon asked.

"Not yet," Phillip responded. "But I have a lead. A solid lead."

"Who is your lead?" Karl implored.

"The intern at the morgue."

Karl stopped walking and placed his hands on Phillip's shoulders. He looked at him directly in the eyes.

"Phillip," he began. "Every day we wait is another day that the shadow of Berlin grows darker. Please, do what you can to get in contact with the coroner."

"We just want to talk with the man," Egon interjected. "We just need to reason with him."

"I'll make sure we have a meeting with the coroner. I promise."

Jurgen sat in a chair in the interrogation room. He was tapping his foot on the stone floor. Stephen, now sitting right side up, was still passed out. His head hung down. While the Gestapo waited for his prisoner to wake up, he wiped his handkerchief over the barrel of his gun. Once it was properly clean, he stood up and returned the weapon back to its holster. He grew bored waiting for Stephen to wake up.

He walked over to the corner of the room where there was a bucket of the prisoner's urine. He picked it up and poured it over his head. Stephen was jolted awake, stunned and gasping for breath. His eyes and wounds stung.

"Ahh," Jurgen said. "So nice of you to finally wake up,"

"What the hell do you want?" Stephen pleaded.

"What is O5?"

"What?"

Jurgen punched him across the face.

"What is O5?"

"Keep punching me, it will help me remember!"

Jurgen walked over to the door and opened it. Two men were standing by the door.

"Gentlemen, please come join us."

They both walked in and pulled out of their pockets brass knuckles. They placed the discreet weapons in their hands.

"Stephen," Jurgen began. "We know you are a member of the resistance group O5."

"If you know what O5 is, why do you keep asking me what it is?"

"We know you are an enemy of Germany."

"And I know you don't have a pecker, Nazi slime."

"Udo? Would you please help our friend here remember who is in charge?"

The guard to Jurgen's left stepped forward and punched Stephen directly in the jaw. Blood immediately began to pour out of his lacerated lip. He spat the blood, along with a tooth, out of his mouth and onto the floor.

"Where does O5 hold its meetings," Jurgen asked.

"In your mother's whorehouse!"

Udo punched Stephen again.

Phillip walked across St. Stephen's square towards the Cathedral. He tried to look like he was minding his own business, but he was the only one in the square. It was the dead of night. He approached the door, the same door that Jorg took him through earlier. He knocked, trying to replicate the same staccato rhythm. There was no answer. He tried again. With every moment that passed, he grew more and more agitated. The cold air began to hurt the insides of his nostrils. He rubbed his fingers through his hair and sighed. He tried the knock again. Finally, the door opened but only a crack.

"Yes?" the voice from inside said. "Can I help you?"

Phillip did not know what to say.

"My name is Phillip Dibbon. I was here the other night."

The door opened a little wider and the young priest stepped through. Once they made eye contact, the priest's eyes grew wide, and his lips curled inside his mouth. Phillip could tell that he was mad. The priest looked around feverishly before grabbing the young reporter by the wrist and pulling him into the church and slamming the door shut.

"You must be seriously deranged!" the young priest said in an angry whisper. "Saying your full name? Knocking over and over?"

"I'm sorry, I just," Phillip tried to find the words.

"Come with me."

The priest walked hastily down the corridor and Phillip followed. They got to the meeting room and now about twice as many people were waiting. Word about O5 was clearly spreading.

Jorg was again at the front of the room, speaking passionately to the assembled crowd. Every few sentences, the supporters in the room would applaud. Phillip stood in the back, watching it all. He was becoming more and more inspired by what he was seeing and hearing.

"This is not about our lives but everyone's," Jörg said to applause. "We need to do what we must and what we can. We know we are not alone in this fight. There are other groups just like us meeting right now and organizing against our oppressors! But the rest of the world turned all of their backs on us! But if we lay down and wait for Roosevelt and Chamberlain to wake up, the war will be over before it was even fought! Spread the word, forcibly open the eyes of your neighbors, let them know the truth of what's going on!"

People applauded and cheered.

"The Nazis know the language of vengeance and retribution better than anyone. Right now, information," Jorg held up his leaflets and letters and presented them to the crowd. "Changing minds, no matter how slowly, is the strongest and most important tool in our arsenal."

Everyone, including Phillip, nodded in agreement. As the meeting came to a close, the attendees grabbed handfuls of leaflets and letters. Like they did in the last meeting, they folded them carefully and stuffed them into their pants' waistlines, their underwear, under their hats, in their boots, or in their bicycle's tires tubing.

Phillip waited in the back as people cleared out. Once everyone left, Jorg approached.

"Good to see you again," Jorg said.

"Likewise," Phillip replied. "We need to continue our discussion about Sindelar."

"I thought you had everything you needed, "Jorg responded.

"I did, but there are people close to me who need something more."

"Who are you referring to?"

"People who knew Sindelar. They're worried about what will happen if what's in those leaflets spread."

"Why should they be worried about the truth getting out?"

"How many guns and tanks do you have?" Phillip stared at Jorg's face as he spoke. "You said it yourself, Jorg. "Vengeance and retribution is the language the Nazis speak best. You, me, the people here tonight. We're not soldiers. No army is going to come and save us. As you said, Roosevelt and Churchill are sitting on their hands. The French? Do you think they'll save us? They all will let us rot in a concentration camp like they're letting the Jews rot."

"Phillip, what are you talking about?"

"Right now, Sindelar's death is listed as suicide. That means he can't have a funeral. If the people out there can't say goodbye to him, it will allow rumors spread. Even though you're telling people the truth, the Nazis could seize on this and take it to the extreme."

"We need more people on our side," Jorg said softly. "We need people to know the facts and know the truth about what is going on."

"People don't care about facts, Jorg. If they did,

they would have heard the drums a few years ago. People just want to live their lives. And your plan could completely backfire and get us all killed. What good is a resistance if we don't have what we need to even resist."

Jorg was taken aback by what his new friend was saying.

"So what do you want me to do?" Jorg and Phillip shared eye contact.

"Do what's right for everyone and it will ultimately help our cause. Sometimes you resist tyranny by smashing windows. Other times, you resist tyranny by manipulating it."

Jorg walked out of the church and grabbed his bicycle. He jogged a little bit down the street and jumped on it. He made his way to the hospital. As he approached, he began to dismount the bike and rode it while he stood on one of the peddles. He got to the morgue's entrance and reached into his pockets and grabbed his keys.

He hopped off the bike, left it against a tree, and he fumbled with his keys as he tried to open the door. Once inside, he made his way to Dr. Quester's office. He closed the door behind him and only turned on the desk lamp. He tried to be as secretive as he possibly could be. He searched through the papers on the desk and then in the filing cabinet.

As he searched, he heard footsteps coming down the hallway. He froze. He waited for a moment as he felt his heart beat faster.

He took a breath as the footsteps grew fainter. He smiled to himself and continued to search for the Sindelar file.

He looked through the piles of papers and the drawers, and then he found it. It was shoved inside another file in the very back of the bottom drawer of the cabinet. He pulled out the pages, slid them inside of his sock leg, and left the office. He got back on his bike and went home.

Phillip was not paying attention to the morning editorial meeting at the Krone. He was sitting in the back of the room doodling in his notebook.

"Phillip," his editor said. His head came up from his drawing and looked at his superior. "What do you have?"

He honestly did not have any stories to pitch and his mind was completely blank. He thought briefly about saying something about the coroner's office releasing an updated autopsy, but he worried about Jorg's safety if he said anything.

"I wouldn't mind doing a follow up on the

pharmacy robbery," he said finally.

"What's the follow up to that one?"

"Not sure, just a hunch that it might be worth making some calls on."

That ended up being his assignment. He walked out of the conference room deflated. He did not want to be at work that day. He sat down at his desk and stared at his typewriter. He lifted the levers and turned the dial to feed the paper through the machine. Then, he lined up the page to sit just right. He fed in a piece of paper and his hands fell onto the desk with a bit of a thud. He was hoping that words would just magically appear on the page, releasing him of the duty of having to write his story.

He found the energy to grab his satchel shoulder bag and slowly left the newsroom. As he left the building and stepped out onto the busy sidewalk, he saw a swastika banner hanging from a light pole. He stopped for a moment and gazed at it. He thought about what it would have been like for his great-grandfather, a man who fought against Napoleon's invading armies, to see what had happened to his country. He thought about the horror he would feel to see the emblem of a foreign power flying across the now-former capital of Austria. Those empathic feelings turned his stomach.

Jorg's apartment was small and quaint. The bookshelves around his apartment were mostly bare, except for the medical textbooks and the dust outlines showing where books used to sit. All of his books were now stored away, hidden in a box in the back of his closet. They were books about socialism, Karl Marx, and the Russian Revolution.

The medical student sat on the edge of his bed as he looked over the autopsy report about Matthias Sindelar. As he read it over, line by line, he wondered if Phillip was right. If the public could not mourn his passing, could this particular death be turned into an excuse for the Nazis to decimate all of Austria? Could this cause more people to turn on the resistance instead of joining it? It is all possible, of course. Jorg wondered if changing the death certificate was worth the risk or if he should continue to hope that he was right, instead of Phillip.

Jorg believed, in his heart, that he was doing the right thing by sending out leaflets explaining the truth about how the Nazis stormed the coroner's office and stopped the autopsy. How they might have even been behind his death and that of his fiancee. He felt that spreading the word would help rally people behind O5 and fight the Germans. This was his form of resistance. But he could not get Phillip's words out of his head.

Jorg placed the papers down on his bed and walked

over to his dresser. He picked up a coin and placed it on the knuckle of his thumb and his curved forefinger.

"If it's heads, I continue to spread the word," he said. "Tails, I change the report."

He flipped the coin into the air and caught it. He closed his fingers into a fist and waited a moment before he looked at it. Then, he looked down and saw the figure side of the coin. Tails. He would change the report.

He sat down at his typewriter and loaded in a new death certificate template. He lined up the page to the section asking for "Sir Name." In that section, he typed, S I N D E L A R. He hit the tab key a few times and then lined up the page to "Given Name." There he typed out, M A T T H I A S.

He typed in all the identifying descriptions regarding his height and weight. Then, he got to the section for the cause of death. There, he did not type "suicide," as Doctor Quester wrote on his report.

Jorg kept his eyes on the keyboard as his fingers found the next ten letters. The most important letters he would be typing, A C C I D E N T A L.

As he looked at the page, he could feel his blood pumping through his ears. He nodded and let out a deep and heavy sigh. He moved the page over to the notes section. Jorg explained there how the findings of the toxicology report were similar to other accidental carbon monoxide deaths. How the blood-oxygen levels were not overly saturated with the toxic gas, indicating that the body was still absorbing atmospheric oxygen as opposed to pure amounts of carbon monoxide. But the brain was not receiving enough oxygen causing the victim to slip into a coma and ultimately his death.

He finished the report and pulled the page out of the typewriter, He then repeated the same exercise for Camilla. Before he finished for the night, he took Dr. Quester's report and traced his signature on the new reports that he just created.

The hospital's morgue had no windows. It was extremely cold and unwelcoming for fairly obvious reasons. The walls and floor were covered in tiles, to make it easier to clean. Dr. Harold Quester walked into the morgue and was pleased to find Jorg already in the office and going over paperwork.

"You're here early," Dr. Quester said. He put his briefcase down and walked to the filing cabinet.

"Yes, Herr Doctor. I wanted to get a head start on some of my work today."

"Finding anything interesting?"

"Actually, yes," Jorg replied. "The definitive results of Sindelar's death came in overnight." Jorg made sure not to change the inflection of his voice. Dr. Quester froze. He was told that the blood work had been canceled.

"Good," he said tentatively and turned around slowly. "I'll take care of it."

"I already did, sir," Jorg said with confidence.

"What?"

"I made all the appropriate corrections to the death certificate and took the liberty of filing it with the clerk."

"Let me see the finding, right away!" Dr. Quester's demeanor was turning to panic. Even though Jorg did what he was supposed to do, and was taught to do, this was not an ordinary case where the cause of death was not ordered by the authorities. There was not supposed to be a formal finding of blood work. Sindelar and Camilla were scheduled to be buried in an unmarked grave with the rest of the suicides of the Nazi era.

Jorg found the findings, which he wrote the night before, and handed them to his mentor.

"Is there a problem?" the intern asked.

"None," the doctor said as he looked the report over and sat down in his chair. His head was spinning. He could not focus on what was printed on the page. His mind was inventing so many different scenarios about what would happen once the authorities found out what happened. "No, everything is ok. What did you change on the death certificate."

"The cause of death, Herr Doctor, was clearly accidental. It could not have been suicide."

"Based on what?"

"The oxygen levels in the blood," Jorg pointed out the numbers on the report. "This is concurrent in the previous autopsies you and I have done where carbon monoxide poisoning is the primary culprit."

Dr. Quester's jaw dropped.

"And you've already filed this with the clerk," he asked with a quiver in his voice.

"Yes, sir. I have."

The doctor stood and shook his head.

"Excuse me for a few moments."

He walked into his office and closed the door behind him. He picked up his phone and called Arnold Drazan. The phone rang several times before the attorney answered it.

"Herr Drazan. It's Dr. Quester. We have an issue with the Sindelar case."

Sitting on a park bench for lunch became a habit for him now. He now had to give himself a moment before going back to Kronen Zeitung. He needed to recharge. The world was changing before his eyes and his heart was changing with it. The job he was doing for the paper was no longer a job that he wanted to do. Being a journalist now did not make him feel like he was an important member of a free society, he felt like a cog in the wheel of the Nazi Party. He felt like his paper was merely toeing the party line and an extension of the Reich Ministry of Public Enlightenment and Propaganda.

He wanted to join the resistance fully and completely. He knew that he could not live a lie as a working journalist. He was not a good enough actor to fool the people in his office every single day. He should switch careers so he could still earn a salary and pay his bills. He knew what he was risking if he was discovered by the authorities. But, in his heart of hearts, he wanted to do what he could for O5. He wanted to help them write leaflets. He wanted to help them get the word out to get more recruits for their most just cause.

When he got back to his desk, he did not write his story. He instead wrote his resignation letter. He was brief and to the point. He filed it in his editor's in-box, picked up his bag, and left the newsroom.

He went to a nearby bar and began to drink beer. He flirted with the waitress and his buzz became drunkenness. He ordered more beer and led the other patrons in singing traditional Austrian drinking songs, some German songs, and other popular folk songs.

Phillip wanted to feel alive again. He was drinking

away his frustrations. He was feeling carefree and youthful. As the afternoon turned into the night, more people were showing up. One patron sat next to him and tried to strike up a conversation with him.

"What brings you here, young man," he asked. He was about ten years older than Phillip, his hair was beginning to gray. He wore a black jacket with a collared shirt under it.

"I just quit my job!" Phillip replied enthusiastically.

"Good for you! What's your name," the man held out his hand.

"Dibbon. Phillip Dibbon." They shook hands.

"What did you do, Herr Dibbon?"

"Until this afternoon, I worked for the Krone. I told my son of a bitch of a boss that he could sit on it! I'm free!"

"I've had my fair share of crummy bosses too. So what's next for you?"

Phillip brought his beer stein to his lips and drank the remaining beer in one fell swoop. With foam sticking to his mouth, which he wiped away with his sleeve, he looked at his new friend and smiled.

"I'm going to overthrow the government!" He then held up his empty stein and shouted, "Beer wench! Bring me another!"

"I think you might have had enough, son. Let's get you home so you can sleep it off."

"Oh come now, we're celebrating!"

The waitress came over and looked at Phillip.

"Young Herr," she said. "Your friend is right. It's time for you to head home."

"He's not my friend!" Phillip, in his drunken state, pushed the man away and stood. He stumbled but he managed to keep his balance. "You're not my friend. Don't say that you're my friend. I'm a free man! I'm going to live a free life!"

The waitress, now with the bartender, escorted the former reporter out of the bar and threw him into the street.

"Go home and sleep it off!" the bartender shouted.

Phillip stumbled away and threw his fists around in the air like he was fighting an invisible enemy.

"I am home!" he shouted. "This is my home!"

He started walking down the street, not sure which way he was going. He was singing a folk song to himself. He was not able to walk in a straight line. He was stumbling all over the sidewalk. He almost stepped into the street more than once.

He passed by a dancehall right when a group of young Nazis, dressed in their uniforms, were leaving. Phillip walked right into one of them.

"Watch where you're going!" one of the Nazis yelled. He grabbed Phillip by the collar and shoved him out of their way.

"He's drunk," another said. They all chuckled and began to walk away.

"Don't walk away from me!" Phillip shouted. "You can't start something and not finish it!"

The group turned and laughed at him. Phillip brought his arms up as if he were a boxer.

"You're drunk go home," one of the Nazis said.

"Come on!" Phillip shouted. "You don't scare me! Or are you a coward?"

"Is this guy serious?"

"Come on, coward! You don't have a tank to protect you now!"

The Nazi closest to Phillip brought his fist back and punched him across the jaw. He immediately fell to the ground. He crawled into a nearby alley before he passed out. The group of young men walked away laughing at him.

The next morning, Phillip woke up without a clear idea of how or why he was inside an alleyway. His head was pounding and his jaw hurt. He touched his lip, and it was sensitive to the touch. He forced himself to his feet and slowly, he got his bearings. He started to walk, slowly putting one foot in front of the other. He figured out where he was and figured how to get home.

When he got to his apartment, he found the door

unlocked. He pushed it open and looked at the sight before him. His entire apartment was ransacked. A chill came over him. He thought, at first, that he had been robbed.

He immediately started to look for his personal possessions. He was trying to figure out if anything was stolen. His books were all over the floor. His desk drawers were open and papers were scattered everywhere. In his bedroom, his clothes were pulled off their hangers and all the pockets turned inside out. The only things that seemed to be missing were his notes and writings.

His feelings of violation transformed into sheer panic. He stood up straight and his breathing quickened. His heart started to beat so fast, it felt like his ribs were struggling to keep it in his chest. His eyes shot back from left to right at a frantic pace.

He knew he was in trouble.

Walter Nausch sat down for breakfast at a German cafe with his wife. Giving up familiar food was difficult for them. Switzerland might have been home to many German speakers and native Germans, but it still was not home. The waiter brought them a pot of coffee in a French press along with semmel with butter. The waiter also placed that morning's newspaper, folded, at the edge of the table.

Walter picked it up and immediately started crying.

"What is it?" his wife asked. "What's wrong?"

Walter showed her the newspaper. There it was, in black and white, a headline he never thought he would be able to read. "Death of Matthias Sindelar Ruled Accidental."

Max Uhrmann walked down the hallway of the prosecutor's office in haste. He wanted to see Arnold Drazan. He got near his office and the secretary stood. He walked right past her and barged his way into the young lawyer's office. Forced to interrupt his work, Drazan looked up and knew what this impromptu meeting was going to be about.

"Do you have something you want to tell me?" Urhmann asked sternly as he approached his desk.

"I only found out the same way you did."

"I do not like surprises."

"I'm just as surprised as you are."

"How did this happen?"

"Apparently there was conflicting evidence in a medical exam report. An intern thought he was going above and beyond the call of duty and corrected the report himself," Drazen explained.

"An intern?"

"He was only doing what he thought was right."

"Well. Now, I need to do what I think is right."

Max stood up and walked to the door.

"We'll be in touch."

J urgen allowed Stephen, his prisoner, to have a break from the torture and the interrogation. He allowed him to drink some clean water and eat some fresh bread. Stephen had difficulty chewing because he was now missing some teeth.

"Tell me something," Jurgen decided to ask finally.

"What?"

"Why do you oppose the Reich?"

"Why do you support it?"

Jurgen looked at him and then at a crease in the wall.

"I love my country and I love my people. I love being able to support both by helping weed out dissidents like you. I know that they are right when they say that we are the master race. We are the people who took down the Roman Empire, after all."

Stephan took a sip of water and then looked at Jurgen.

"But you couldn't beat France a few years ago?"

Jurgen walked over to him and kicked him square

in the stomach. Over and over again. After five or six strong, swift kicks in the abdomen, he grabbed him by the hair and pulled his head back while he was gasping for air. Jurgen looked the prisoner in the face and spat on it.

Jurgen stood and pulled a knife out of his pocket. Then he grabbed Stephan's left leg and sliced right through the man's Achilles tendon. The scream of anguish was intense.

Jurgen moved on to the other leg.

"Please don't!" The blade entered the flesh and cut through.

Blood poured onto the floor. Stephen's legs, now useless, felt like a fire burning.

"What do you know about O5?"

"Why God?! Why?!"

"What do you know about O5?" The edge of the blade was now on the inside of Stephan's small toe.

"His name is Jorg," he said panting. "He's in charge. Jorg Unterreiner."

Jurgen removed the blade and wiped the blood away from it with his sleeve.

"If this information ends up being fake, I will personally sign the order for your mother and her mother to go to Dachau."

Phillip barely slept. He thought quite a bit about what it would be like to wake up on the first morning after leaving the Krone. As his eyes saw the light of the sun coming through the window, the feelings he felt were nothing like what he imagined. Instead of feeling free and joyful, he instead felt anxious and nervous.

He got out of bed, walked into the bathroom, and stared at himself in the mirror. He reached over to the tub and turned on the shower. He thought about what he should do about money, what he should do about O5, whether or not he should get out of the country, his family, everything. Shaving was more difficult because of all the emotions he was feeling.

After getting dressed, he put on his coat and made his way towards the morgue. He wanted to speak to Jorg about O5, where he saw the resistance efforts going, any next steps, and also to just clear his head.

Once he got to the morgue, he tried the door and discovered that it was locked. He looked at his watch and was surprised that no one was in the office yet. He shrugged his shoulders and started to walk away. He saw two figures approaching him.

"Young Herr," one of them said. Phillip immediately recognized the two men as Gestapo officers.

"What business do you have with the morgue?"

"Why do you ask?" Phillip was apprehensive.

"Just answer the question, what business do you have with the morgue?"

"I don't have to answer your questions. I'm leaving."

"Wait. Papers please." The two Gestapo stopped Phillip from walking away and pushed him against the wall of the hallway. One of them wrapped his hand around his throat while the other grabbed his bag and emptied its contents onto the floor. "What business do you have with the morgue?"

"Look at this," the other officer said holding up an O5 leaflet.

"You'll be coming with us." As Phillip screamed in protest and begged anyone who could hear for help, the two Gestapo dragged him away. Phillip's pleas for mercy went unanswered.

S hut him up!" Jurgen shouted.

But Philipp could not stop screaming. A Gestapo was in the process of pulling his fingernails out of him with a pair of pliers. Both of his hands were in agony. He could not bend his fingers at all.

"Please God!" he shouted as his knees shook

uncontrollably. He was tied to a chair in a room with a chain hanging from the ceiling. The room smelled like mold. There was no sunlight. Phillip lost track of how long he was in the room. He just knew that he was in excruciating pain.

"I said, shut him up," Jurgen demanded. Another Nazi punched him across the face. As Philipp sat there, weeping, he managed to silence himself. He looked up at Jurgen, his eyes pleading for mercy. He was visibly terrified beyond his wildest imagination by the thought of more pain. He looked down at his hands, seeing all ten fingers deformed and red. He then looked at his lap and noticed that he had soiled himself.

"I don't care why you decided to act so stupidly against your country," Jurgen said. "Your name is Phillip Dibbon, is it not? That's what your identification says."

"Yes." Phillip was confused. He was having difficulty getting his words out.

"Did you, or did you not, say that you were planning on overthrowing the government?"

"What?"

A guard punched him across the face.

"We have a report against you that you said that you were going to overthrow the government."

"I don't know what you're talking about!"

The guard punched him again. Blood was pouring

out of his forehead and his lips. Tears were streaming uncontrollably down his face.

"You are a member of O5! You are an enemy of the German people! I want to know who else is working with you."

Philipp's lips trembled and he could feel his jaw muscles struggle to find the correct position in order to form actual words.

"I don't know their names."

Jurgen looked at his subordinate who immediately understood what his next move should be. The Nazi stood behind the prisoner and placed both hands on Phillip's neck. Jurgen looked at Phillip's panicked face and smiled in sadistic glee.

"Maybe we should help you remember."

The guard pressed his forefingers into the soft flesh below Phillip's ears, right behind his jaw. He pushed in hard. To Phillip, it felt like his cranium was being pushed away from his neck. His eyes opened wide and his mouth fell open.

"Give me a name!"

Phillip could only make noises of agony.

"Just one fucking name!"

After nearly a minute of the torment, Jurgen allowed his prisoner a bit of a reprieve.

"I know you don't want to feel any more pain, do

you?" Phillip shook his head. "Then all this can end and you just need to give me a name."

"Grunwald," he muttered. It was the first name he could think of. It was the family name of a childhood friend.

"Grunwald?" Jurgen asked as he pulled a pack of cigarettes out of his pocket. He pulled one out, placed it between his lips. He then took out his lighter and lit it while inhaling the smoke. The blaze illuminated his face. He then pulled it out and placed it between Phillip's lips who took a long, meaningful drag. "And where can I find this, Grunwald?"

"He's a student at the University. I don't know which one. He's in charge of O5. That's all I know."

Jurgen looked at the guard. He gave him a nod letting him know that the torture was over, for now.

"And tell me this," he asked. "Who is Jorg Unterreiner?"

"I don't know," Phillip lied.

Jurgen took the cigarette and extinguished it on the back of his prisoner's hand.

"Maybe we should help you remember."

Officials for Austria Wein were hastily planning a public memorial for Matthias Sindelar, now that they were legally able to honor their fallen hero. Camilla's remains were being sent back to her family in Italy for burial.

The team commissioned the construction of a memorial headstone for Matthias. What was presented was simple, modern, and, according to team officials, exemplified Matthias' majesty as a player. The bulk of the stone was made of black onyx. In the center of the small memorial, there was a copper engraving of his likeness. His hair slicked back, his gaze looking into eternity. Below, his signature, stitched out of brass. On either side of the stone were two lanterns with candles which would be aflame for all eternity. In between, directly in the center, a football carved out of marble.

Matthias' funeral was planned for that Friday afternoon in St. Stephen's Cathedral. Archbishop Theodor Innitzer wanted to preside, but he was still secluded away at the seminary.

As the bells of the great hall rang, signaling the call to worship, and the startled birds flew away, the doors to the sanctuary opened. One by one, ever so slowly, people began to trickle in with tears slowly streaming down their faces. Some were distant family, some were friends, all were fans of the Paper Man.

The pews began to fill, row after row. Some people arrived after the service had already started. A few of those people were able to find a seat, those who could not simply stood along the side. The large cathedral was completely packed with mourners. All in all, twenty-thousand people were there, all wanting to say thank you, to say goodbye, to ask God to bless his soul. For ninety minutes each week, for more than a decade, they had witnessed concertos and symphonies being composed before their eyes by the Mozart of Football in stadiums across Austria and Europe. He made his team, his city, and his nation proud. Now, at his funeral, this was the least his fans could do for the man who brought them so much joy, so much pride, and so much inexplicable exuberance.

The casket was made of the finest oak, coated in wax for protection from the elements. A wreath of flowers adorned it at its head. Ever since Hitler took over Germany and began to expand the nation's borders, Nazi imagery was everywhere, including inside churches. Many people were buried in coffins with swastikas engraved on them. At Matthias' funeral, no such imagery was present.

Karl Sesta stood before the congregation to give the eulogy. He had notes written out on an envelope. But when he stood at the pulpit, his words escaped him. He placed his notes on the pulpit and glanced over at the coffin. His eyes welled up with tears. He could not see what he had written. He wanted to say how Matthias had made him a better soccer player. How he always strived for excellence. How he was a born competitor. Instead, the only thing he was able to talk about was how much his friendship meant to him.

"God puts a few men like Matthias on this Earth once in a generation. It will be a long time before we see another giant of the sporting world be the kind of champion that he was. Sindi was my friend. He was my friend from the beginning, through our careers and until his passing. And when I see him again, he will, then too, be my friend."

He then lowered his head, his face turned red as he struggled to hold back his tears but was unable to. He grabbed his papers, his hands shook as he folded them and placed them back in his jacket pocket. He slowly walked down the stairs and back into his seat next to his wife. They embraced and she let him cry for a few moments.

After a closing prayer, a processional led the congregation out of the Cathedral and to Zentralfriedhof Cemetery. All of the twenty thousand in attendance walked slowly across the cobblestone streets of St. Stephen's Square, through the historic Viennese streets. They followed the small entourage of the clergy to what would be the final resting place of Matthias Sindelar. Some people who did not attend the service stood in solemn respect as they watched the funeral procession pass by. Some wiped away tears, others gave their hero one final ovation. A group of Wien supporters sang one more song to their hero and captain: "We love you Sindi, we always will."

Once at the gravesite, the priests, in unison, blessed the ground with Holy Water. They performed the sign of the cross over the coffin, and each person in attendance, in turn, crossed themselves. The pallbearers then proceeded to lower the casket into the ground.

"In nomine Patis, et filii, et Spiritus Sancti," they recited.

Karl, Egon, and Gustav watched, holding their wives' hands, wiping away the tears from their cheeks, as the first few grains of the earth covered the coffin. As the service finished, people began to leave the site one by one. Each wanting to pay their final respects to a man they so admired.

"Goodbye, my friend," Karl said.

"I will miss you," Egon whispered.

Before they left, they each took a moment to pray silently at the gravesite. Karl placed his hand on the headstone and looked at the engraving of Matthias' face.

"A part of me wonders what he would have thought of this," he said.

"You think it's a little much?" Egon replied.

"I think he would have said, 'What's the big deal? I was just trying to do my best.'"

"His best was better than all of our bests put together," Gustav said. "That's why this is here."

"I know."

As they walked together towards where their wives were waiting, they did not notice the black Mercedes on the other side of the cemetery. Gestapo agents were inside the car, watching the solemn proceedings and taking note of everyone in attendance.

Phillip was asleep on the floor of his moldy cell. He thought he was asleep, it was impossible to get comfortable in the conditions he was forced to endure. His fingers still hurt, his muscles ached. His wounds were not healing properly. His clothes were stained with blood. He was exhausted from the torture he was suffering. His body forced his eyes closed to get some rest.

But his slumber was interrupted by the sound of the giant metal locks on the door becoming unhinged and opening.

"Oh God," he said as about a dozen the Nazi guards entered. Phillip instinctively curled up into the fetal position, protecting himself.

"Get up," one of them shouted. Two guards grabbed his arms and forced him to his feet. They started to walk him out of his cell.

"What's going on?" Phillip asked in a panic. "Where are you taking me?"

"Shut up!"

They dragged Phillip out of his cell, his legs dangling behind him. As they carried him down the corridor and down the flight of stairs, he screamed "NO" over and over again. He cried uncontrollably.

He was then forced into a truck with six other prisoners, one of whom was Jorg, who was also beaten severely. Jorg smiled at Phillip.

"We will be remembered as heroes," Jorg said to Phillip.

The hatch was locked and the driver turned on the truck. Jorg reached out to his friend and gave him his hand as comfort.

"Don't be afraid," Jorg whispered. "This will soon be over but our cause will live on."

"I don't want to die," Phillip said through his tears.

"If you didn't convince me to change the death certificate, our cause might have died with us."

The truck stopped at a bend along the Danube River.

"Everyone out," a Nazi shouted while the hatch was lowered. "Out now! Line up over there, let's go!"

As Phillip got out, he looked around and saw four men standing with shotguns slung over their shoulders. He, Jorg, and the other prisoners walked over to a wooden pier. Phillip wanted to keep his eyes open to see the beauty of Vienna one last time. He glanced over at Jorg who held his chin high, shoulders back and his eyes kept shut.

"I refused to live in fear," Jorg shouted. "I do not fear death as death by the hands of a tyrant is a proud moment!"

Jorg turned around and opened his eyes. He opened his hands to the firing squad and smiled.

"You are forgiven," he said. "For you know not what you do!"

Phillip gazed at his friend and smiled at him, tears still rolling down his cheek.

"Let's shut the scum up," the Nazi commander shouted. "Ready! Aim! Fire!"

The Nazi executioners fired their weapons at the prisoners. Their now lifeless bodies fell into the Danube and floated away with the current.

Karl sat in the bleachers of the Praterstadion and gazed out over the pitch. He remembered his days of playing with his friend, Sindi. He felt the cool breeze of the morning air against his face. As he looked out over the field, he felt his spirit. He remembered seeing him run free, fooling defenders out of position, and scoring goals that no one else could score. He closed his eyes, took in a deep breath, and remembered the sound of the crowd erupt in a jovial cheer loud enough to reach Heaven.

His brief meditation was interrupted when Rudolf slapped him on the shoulder. The groundskeeper sat down next to him and looked out at the pitch as well.

"He really changed the game for the better," Rudolf said. He knew what Karl was daydreaming about.

"He made me a better player," Karl replied.

"He might have, but you were a great player too, Karl." The player smiled humbly. "On and off the pitch, he did what he had to do. Always the right thing."

Karl looked at the groundskeeper.

"It's difficult to do the right thing even if it feels like the wrong thing. Sometimes when you're doing the right thing, you have your doubts. Matthias knew these days would be dark," Rudolf's words trailed off into a whisper and did not complete his thought.

"Rudolf," Karl said softly. "How do you think Matthias died?"

The groundskeeper stood and smiled at Karl. He held his shoulder and gazed out at the pitch one more time.

"Matthias passed away because God needed him."

Rudolf walked up the stairs and into the stadium. Karl watched him walk away and nodded to himself.

He stood and buttoned his jacket. He walked to the pitch and along the sidelines to the dressing room. There, Karl found Matthias' locker and looked inside of it. He knew that in the generations to come, other players would use this locker. But none would be as influential on or off the pitch as his friend and idol, Matthias Sindelar.

CODA

About eight months after Matthias died, Hitler invaded Poland which formally started World War II. Six years later, in 1945, when it was clear that Germany was going to be defeated, Hitler committed suicide in an underground bunker, signaling an end to the war in Europe. As part of the peace treaty, Austria was reinstated as an independent republic, and Germany was divided into two nations, East and West Germany.

While the war was raging, FIFA canceled its quadrennial international tournament, the World Cup. It was not staged again until the summer of 1950 in Brazil. Neither Austria nor the two Germanys participated. Austrian football officials claimed its squad was too inexperienced and opted to withdraw from qualification. Neither East nor West Germany was admitted to FIFA until after the tournament ended.

By the time the 1954 World Cup was staged in Switzerland, both Austria and West Germany qualified and sent teams. The two nations met in the Semi-Finals Round on June 30 in Basel's St. Jakob Stadium. The West Germans had Sepp Heberger as their manager. The Austrians were led by Walter Nausch.

The West Germans would go on to win that match 6 to 1 and ultimately go on to win the World Cup trophy. The Austrians came in third place. When the triumphant West Germans came home to a heroes' welcome, Chancellor Konrad Adenauer announced to the crowd, "Finally, we are somebody again!"

It was a call not only to the world that the Germans were athletically formidable, but as a people, the ghost of Adolf Hitler was being lifted and they had something to be proud of again.

In subsequent years, Germany would win a total of four World Cups. Austria has yet to win one.

The International Federation of Football History & Statistics named Matthias Sindelar the best Austrian soccer player of the 20th Century.

It seems that the glory of the Wunderteam died with him, The Paper Man.

ABOUT THE AUTHOR

DAVID JAMES ROBERTS is a writer, journalist, documentarian and life-long soccer fan. He lives in Tacoma, Washington, with his wife, daughter, and two dogs.

www.ingramcontent.com/pod-product-compliance
Lightning Source LLC
Chambersburg PA
CBHW070513310726

48976CB00002BA/427